"Another drink for you, groom-to-be?"

Distracted, Jonathan glanced at her. "Oh. Thank you, Mary Anne. When you come back–"

But she was already walking away, leaving the crowd behind.

This was the ms glass and her o t was unattended cabernet and po h the uncapped vial of potion against her palm, let it run into his glass with the wine.

She poured herself some merlot and took a sip to steady her nerves.

"Ah, thank you, Mary Anne."

A masculine hand took the second glass from her hand.

Mary Anne did not release it. "No, that's for–" She gripped the glass tightly.

Appalled, she felt the stem break, the foot come off in her hand.

Graham Corbett looked in astonishment from the piece she held to the one he held. Then in a mock salute, he lifted his part of the glass to his lips and drank deeply.

Dear Reader,

One of life's most frustrating realities, which most people learn at an early age, is that not all love is returned in equal measure. Most of us learn young that we can fall madly in love with someone who doesn't know we're alive. The girl falls in love with the high school football player, but he likes her best friend…and so on.

In the realm of legends, fairy tales and Harry Potter, one of the solutions to this problem has been the love potion. Of course, it's in no way a foolproof answer. Though all is fair in love and war, we want to be loved without having to resort to witchcraft. And as to enchanted drafts, the wrong people sometimes drink them.

I hope you enjoy reading of love potions in a contemporary context and meeting Mary Anne Drew and Graham Corbett, who can both at least comfort themselves with the thought that love potions don't work anyway.

Wishing you happiness and all good things always.

Sincerely,

Margot Early

THE THINGS WE DO FOR LOVE
FOR LOVE
Margot Early

TORONTO • NEW YORK • LONDON
AMSTERDAM • PARIS • SYDNEY • HAMBURG
STOCKHOLM • ATHENS • TOKYO • MILAN • MADRID
PRAGUE • WARSAW • BUDAPEST • AUCKLAND

Recycling programs
for this product may
not exist in your area.

ISBN-13: 978-0-373-71546-6
ISBN-10:   0-373-71546-3

THE THINGS WE DO FOR LOVE

ABOUT THE AUTHOR

Margot Early has written stories since she was twelve years old. She has published more than twenty books with Harlequin Books; her work has been translated into nine languages and sold in sixteen countries. Ms. Early lives high in Colorado's San Juan Mountains with two German shepherds and several other pets, including snakes and tarantulas. She enjoys the outdoors, dance and spinning dog hair.

Books by Margot Early

HARLEQUIN SUPERROMANCE
766—WHO'S AFRAID OF THE MISTLETOE?
802—YOU WERE ON MY MIND
855—TALKING ABOUT MY BABY
878—THERE IS A SEASON
912—FOREVER AND A BABY
1333—HOW TO GET MARRIED
1357—A FAMILY RESEMBLANCE
1376—WHERE WE WERE BORN
1401—BECAUSE OF OUR CHILD
1436—GOOD WITH CHILDREN

HARLEQUIN AMERICAN ROMANCE
1229—HOLDING THE BABY

A man who believed me to be a witch once asked me,
quite gravely, if I'd put a spell on him.
I thought it a remarkable question and told him,
"Not on you."
This book is for him.

CHAPTER ONE

Logan, West Virginia

MARY ANNE DREW was at her desk at *The Logan Standard and the Miner* when Cameron brought the news. Cameron, who was Mary Anne's first cousin and best friend, grabbed a chair and straddled it, facing Mary Anne. "They're engaged."

Mary Anne did not ask who. She said, "No," in a way that was sort of like a prayer.

Her face showing that she knew she was causing pain, Cameron said, "Yes. Angie and her friends were drinking martinis at the Face last night and Rhonda waited on them, and she told me that's the news. She doesn't have a ring yet, though."

It couldn't be true. Mary Anne smothered her feelings in a cascade of repetitions of this thought.

She'd been in love with Jonathan Hale for four years, ever since he'd arrived in Logan from Cincinnati to manage the public radio station, WLGN. She'd never experienced anything like it. At first, she'd thought nothing of the tall dark-haired man with his wire-rimmed glasses and matter-of-fact manner. Yes, she'd been impressed with the time he'd spent working overseas as a correspondent for Reuters. She knew he'd seen dreadful things in war zones, things he didn't discuss. Then, one day when she'd come in to record an essay, he'd sat listening and watching her with brooding intensity. Afterward, he'd said, "That was good work, Mary Anne. I'm going to try to get it out to as many other stations as I can."

She'd looked into his blue eyes and she had felt something that was almost like an arrow through the heart. She'd never understood where that image of Eros had come from until that moment; she'd been nailed by the arrows of Aphrodite's son. The sheer force of the experience convinced her that Jonathan Hale was meant to be hers.

She believed it still.

Cameron asked, "Are you okay?"

"Sure."

No, she wasn't okay! She was dying. How could she go through the next five minutes, let alone the rest of her life, knowing that Jonathan Hale planned to wed that tacky and *tiny* thing, Angie Workman, who was manager of the Blooming Rose, the closest thing Logan had to a boutique. To bolster the notion that this news meant nothing to her, she said, "Aren't you working?"

Cameron was director of the Logan County Women's Resource Center, located next door to the newspaper office.

"Coffee break. A client's mother came in and told her marriage is for life and she's ashamed that her own daughter should seek a divorce from the fine man who broke three bones in her face last week. She wound up by calling yours truly and our legal-aid attorney godless man-haters. I'm cooling off." Cameron switched back to Mary Anne's concerns. "I have a last-chance idea. Just for fun. Not that it will work. But it would be fun to find out if it could work."

Mary Anne studied her cousin. Like Mary Anne, Cameron was blond—or somewhat blond. They had the same light brown hair, which became lighter in the sun. But there the resemblance ended.

Cameron, to Mary Anne's envy, was small. In fact, genes had granted her the kind of body that was currently in vogue—boyishly small hips and a pair of tatas that made men stare. She was a natural athlete who never drove if she could walk, run or ride a bike to get where she needed to go. Her idea of a good time on weekends was leading Women of Strength events for the women from the resource center's shelter. She had a black belt in tae kwon do and was an experienced caver. Mary Anne, on the other hand, knew that her own rear end would benefit from less time in chairs and in the driver's seat of her car.

Cameron was five foot five. Mary Anne was five foot ten. And Mary Anne lived for haute couture—after all, before settling in Logan she had worked for two different women's magazines in New York and could swear that everything in *The Devil Wears Prada* was true. Cameron's clothes came from thrift shops. Mary Anne indulged in highlights, and Cameron wouldn't dream of it. Mary Anne was an editor and reporter for *The Logan Standard and the Miner;* Cameron had the aforementioned challenging job of safeguarding the welfare of women and children.

Being that Cameron had a set of requirements for any man with whom she might be involved, Mary Anne was touched by her cousin's interest in helping her secure Jonathan Hale's affection and desire. Jonathan *nearly* met Cameron's prerequisite for a man ready for marriage. Though he *was* employed and *wasn't* an alcoholic, Mary

Anne doubted he'd ever had therapy, something Cameron insisted all males required. Cameron herself also wanted a man who didn't need to reproduce, who was willing to adopt. "There are plenty of children in the world," Cameron would say. "Children who need good homes."

The truth, Mary Anne knew, was that Cameron had watched her own sister go through an agonizing labor, which concluded with a cesarean section. She had told Mary Anne, *"Never. I will never…"*

Mary Anne liked the idea of having children. No, she *wanted* children. This fact had given her dreams about Jonathan an extra edge of desperation. "What's the last-ditch idea?" she asked Cameron.

Cameron's brown eyes gleamed, looking almost black. "A love potion."

This suggestion was *soooo* Cameron. You would think, Mary Anne often reflected, that a woman who heard heinous stories of domestic abuse, rape and what-have-you every day, would have surgically removed every last romantic cell in her body. Cameron claimed that this was the case. It just wasn't. And whenever Cameron *did* become romantic, it was things like this…

The fortune teller at the state fair, who'd told Cameron she would marry a dark-haired brown-eyed man; the astrologer who said Cameron would become united with her soul mate through "unconventional means." Chain letters with the message, "You will meet the love of your life within five days of sending this to five people. Do not break the chain!" And, no, Mary Anne was not exempt from Cameron's bizarre schemes.

She forced skepticism to the forefront as she confronted her cousin. "Supposing that such a thing worked—which it *won't*. How are you proposing to obtain it?"

"Paul's mom," Cameron said simply. "The hippie midwife…?"

Paul was what Cameron had instead of a boyfriend—well, she also had a dog, Mary Anne knew. Paul Cureux was a childhood friend who was totally allergic to the idea of commitment—though Mary Anne *had* pointed out that he did have dark hair and brown eyes. Since Cameron was hypercritical of nearly every man she met, she and Paul had made some sort of agreement to give other people the impression that they were a couple. Then Cameron wouldn't have to deal with being pursued by men who'd never had therapy—Paul hadn't, either—and Paul wouldn't have to elude women who wanted to marry him and have his children. It was an arrangement Mary Anne had never understood, especially since Paul—who usually had weekend gigs playing guitar and singing folk music that must have made every woman who heard him know she was alive—seemed to enjoy making women fall in love with him. Mary Anne had once asked her cousin, "Do you have a thing for him?"

"I have a thing for no man," Cameron had replied. "Except the *god*."

She did not mean Paul Cureux. Mary Anne did not think the man to whom Cameron referred was even remotely divine—and neither did she think his psychological house was in the immaculate order Cameron believed it to be. Now, she said, "Paul's mother makes love potions?"

"Yes. Don't you remember? The radio station did that interview with her."

Mary Anne didn't remember. She said, "No," but she didn't mean that she didn't remember. She only meant that she wasn't ready to try anything so silly.

Cameron shrugged. "Your choice. I don't see being single as problematic, but you do. And you've liked this guy for years, though he'd probably make you miserable."

Mary Anne resented the last comment. She knew Cameron found Jonathan Hale far less appealing than she did, but she hated Cameron's insistence that there was a worm in the apple.

Mary Anne simply shook her head. "I have work to do."

Cameron stood up, shaking back her two long braids. "Back to the mines. If you do stop by the radio station, give my regards to the deity."

"I don't speak to that man if I can help it."

When Cameron was gone, Mary Anne sat down in her cubicle and tried to read her piece on the Harvest Tea. She needed to edit it and complete the society page by ten tonight. Her title at the paper was associate editor, and in practice it meant she did a bit of everything. She edited sections on society and the arts, and she covered news and features as they arose.

Barbara Rollins, President of the St. Luke's Catholic Church Altar Society, provided a light sponge cake...

The Harvest Tea just could not compete with the calamity of Jonathan Hale's engagement. Though Jonathan always treated Mary Anne respectfully, he didn't seem to notice her as a woman. Which might be appropriate in someone else's boyfriend. Which he was.

Maybe Cameron was right. Maybe it was worth trying one last insane thing before it was too late. The love potion wouldn't work. Mary Anne did remember the interview with Clare Cureux, though Cameron was wrong about the focus. Jonathan Hale's focus had been rural health-care providers. Mary Anne, herself, had heard him give a firm negative to the questions of Graham Corbett, Logan's insufferable radio talk-show host, who believed he'd single-handedly put Logan County, West Virginia, on the map. Jonathan had said, "She did not mention the love potions, and I didn't ask."

A love potion was a ridiculous idea. But Mary Anne wondered if she could find a pretext for dropping in at the radio station. *Are they really engaged?* Maybe the rumor was false. She thought for a minute, then rose from her desk, pulling on her gray wool blazer and slinging her leather handbag over a shoulder. Hurrying past the office of the editor in chief, she gave him a wave, glad he was on the phone and couldn't ask where the hell she thought she was going. No need to fabricate a meeting of the Daughters of the American Revolution.

She hurried down the stairs of the brick building and outside. Fall was in the air, the smell of dried leaves, a brisk wind, no more sweltering summer days that made her hair limp. She stepped to the curb, looked both ways and waited for a pickup truck to pass before running across Main Street in front of an approaching stream of cars. She passed the soda fountain and hurried into the historic brick structure next door, the Embassy Building, which housed WLGN.

Don't let it be true, she thought again. Maybe Cameron had the wrong information about Jonathan and Angie.

As she reached the radio station's glass door, a man swung it open to hold it for her.

Mary Anne felt a rush of distaste, which she hoped showed on her face.

The man who had opened it stood six feet tall and wore his gold-streaked brown hair on the long side, so that it curled around his collar, waving back from his forehead. Frequently, people mistook him for the actor John Corbett, but Graham Corbett was not even related. *Dr. Graham Corbett.* Doctor as in Ph.D., not M.D. Though she knew he did see clients two days a week for counseling, Mary Anne still found Graham Corbett's use of *Doctor* before his name to be just one more affectation. No doubt if he ever learned that Cameron referred to him as a deity, he'd build a temple in his own honor.

"Ah," he said, "the woman with an ass made for radio."

Mary Anne paused to give him a smile of sweet acidity. "And I thought *you* were the ass made for radio."

"My angel," he said, "how is the life of the has-been beauty editor and hard-biting reporter of local fashion shows?"

"I can't wait till someone writes the unauthorized biography," she said, "of you." It lacked the power of her previous comeback, and she knew better than to respond to Graham Corbett at all. She should have remembered that his show was on this afternoon and that he always arrived a half hour early, punctual as a Rolex. Without waiting for his reaction, she stepped past him and into the station. Through the glass window of the recording studio, she could see Jonathan Hale interviewing a coal miner who had black lung disease and silicosis. Mary Anne had heard Jonathan talking about the feature only the day before. He was the station manager, but Logan was a small place, even if it was the county seat, and Mary Anne couldn't imagine Jonathan ever completely abandoning reporting.

His eyes flickered at her briefly through the glass as she passed, and she responded with a little nod, then went to the computer terminal where she knew the archives were stored. Not because she *needed* anything from the archives but because that way she could pretend to have a reason for her appearance.

"To what do we owe this visit?"

Good grief, Graham the Sham had followed her! She said, "Isn't there some other person whose day you'd rather ruin?"

"Absolutely not. I have some news for the society editor of *The Logan Standard and the Miner. East of the Rockies* magazine has named me one of the country's most eligible bachelors, and *People* has chosen me one of their fifty most beautiful people."

"They'll need a two-page spread just for your fat head. Please go away." Without glancing at him, she sat down at the terminal to see if there was anything online about the history of the Logan County Harvest Tea. There wouldn't be, but that did not matter.

Graham Corbett crouched beside her to stage-whisper, "They're engaged."

Somebody's half-finished latte sat in a paper cup beside the terminal like an accident waiting to happen. "Oops!" She knocked it off the desk, but he sprang back in time—catching the cup.

She did glance at him then.

He winked, gave her the grin that Cameron called "so appealing" and finally left her, tossing the coffee cup in a trash can on his way.

Mary Anne did not watch him go. Instead, she reflected that if he knew *anything* about her, he wouldn't have tried to impress her with his mention as a most eligible bachelor, never mind *People*—if that was what he'd been doing. She detested celebrity, thought that even journalists only remained dignified if they kept out of its limelight. *Nobody* became famous and retained his dignity. Graham Corbett, as far as she was concerned, was no exception. He *was,* however, becoming famous, his voice as familiar to many people as Garrison Keillor's, and his following stronger than Dr. Laura's. He'd been interviewed on several major television network talk shows already.

She looked toward the recording booth, seeing Jonathan's compassionate expression as he interviewed the coal miner. Being a journalist was different. Jonathan wasn't a celebrity and never would be, even if he someday won a Pulitzer. He was interested in *other* people, in things outside himself.

She had no idea what Cameron saw in Graham Corbett. But, as for Jonathan... Oh, hell, a love potion couldn't possibly work. But it might be kind of fun to try. She pushed away from the computer console, met Jonathan's eyes for one brief electric moment through the glass of the recording booth and as she left the studio reached in her purse for her cell phone to call Cameron.

BACK AT THE WOMEN'S resource center, Cameron resumed dealing with the details of her work. Calling a plumber to fix pipes in the safe house. Phrasing an ad for the newspaper inviting volunteers to train for the helpline. Checking in with the woman who was presently covering the helpline.

Cameron did her turn on the helpline, too. She knew

she was reasonably good at counseling women in trouble, getting them to take advantage of the center's resources. But every time a woman finally made the decision to leave a partner, Cameron felt so much empathy it was as if she, herself, had endured the ordeals. The husband who disassembled the car to prevent his wife from using it to flee. The cop boyfriend who sat with his service revolver, threatening suicide, in front of the single mother and her three-year-old. Then, there were the calls from men. Threats against her, every employee of the women's resource center, the ex-spouses and ex-girlfriends, the runaway wife, the volunteer.

Graham Corbett, Cameron reflected again, would be the perfect man for her. He was kind on his show, and he gave damned good advice. No way could Cameron imagine him turning into a controlling, possessive type. And he was smart.

Cameron suspected that Graham had the hots for Mary Anne. She'd felt the currents running between them. She even wondered if Mary Anne felt it, too, but was in denial, too fixated on Jonathan. Besides, Mary Anne's father was an actor and musician, an attractive celebrity whose exploits had been covered in international tabloids, a big deal. Mary Anne detested this, and she was never going to go for a man who lived and worked in the public eye.

The love potion had been a fun idea. But a deep part of Cameron badly wanted Mary Anne to succeed with Jonathan, for the simple reason that she herself wanted the chance to date and get to know Graham Corbett—who clearly preferred her cousin.

She should forget the radio star.

Her cell phone rang and she looked at the screen.

Mary Anne.

Cameron smiled and answered, wondering if she was going to learn that her cousin was willing to try a love potion after all.

"WHAT ARE YOU KEEPING those for?" obstetrician David Cureux asked his ex-wife. He had followed Clare into her basement to discover an entire bookcase stocked with foam meat trays. Those were not the only things stored in the basement. There were old magazines, including every copy of *Midwifery Today* ever printed, a stash of gift boxes that took up twenty-four cubic feet of space, the infamous box of rubber bands, another of twisty ties. The woman never threw anything away, but for the life of him David had no idea what she planned to do with those meat trays.

"We'll need these things when it all falls apart," she said.

It, David knew from long and turbulent experience with this woman, was civilization as they knew it. She'd raised two children, who now spoke with a sort of hushed horror of growing up amidst the ominous predictions of a woman they still believed to be a seer, even though they'd finally learned to tune out her prognostications of global disaster.

"I guess you could put them together with duct tape and build yourself a house," he reflected of the meat trays. "Or a coliseum."

"Never mind that. Let's move these upstairs."

These were more than twenty boxes too heavy for the sixty-eight-year-old woman to carry up the cellar steps by herself. They contained telephone directories for the years 1968 to 2005. Not just phone directories that had belonged to Clare, but most of the discarded phone directories for the state of West Virginia—or so David suspected.

"I have to get this done," Clare said, referring to the delivery of the boxes to recycling, which her ex-husband had promised to do with his pickup truck. Clare was reluctant to part with them, but she'd realized that every issue of *Birth Journal* could no longer be kept upstairs. So those magazines were coming downstairs and the phone books would have to leave. "We need to hurry. Someone's coming about a love potion."

A person who knew Clare less well would draw one of the following conclusions: One, she'd made a previous appointment with someone who wanted a love potion. Or two, she'd received a phone message or written message asking her to be home at a particular time to greet a customer interested in a love potion.

David, however, understood that Clare simply "knew" someone was going to come by. Enough people approached her about love potions that it wouldn't be a huge coincidence for her to receive an unannounced visitor requesting one. If such a person arrived in the next few minutes, David would chalk it up to the popularity of his ex-wife's brand of snake oil. Their lives had been full of these instances of Clare supposedly "knowing" things were going to happen. Like the time she'd made them pack up from fishing because Bridget had broken her arm. "Bridget's been hurt. We have to go home," she'd said.

He'd found these announcements aggravating, because she always expected him to act on them. And coincidence had made her nearly always right.

If it wasn't coincidence, there was a scientific explanation of which he was unaware. Whenever he told her that, Clare said matter-of-factly, "Of course, there is."

Clare's point of view was that she had "the sight," but that there was a scientific explanation for this gift.

Nonetheless, David's physician's mind did not stretch to encompass love potions that worked. The love potions were snake oil, and they appeared to "work" because people who were so determinedly in love that they would try such things could often get their way anyhow. And then there was the placebo effect, with all its variations, including the power of positive thinking. The strength of human belief could account for the supposed "success" of the love potions.

David hefted a box of phone books. On the off chance that a victim was on her way—usually it was women who went in for love potions—he preferred not to meet the person. Or be seen anywhere around Clare at the time. His city council seat was up for election again, and the council was having credibility problems as it was; damned if he'd let association with a dispenser of love draughts scupper his chances. He told his ex-wife, "You might think of me."

"I do," she said, misunderstanding. "You need the exercise."

"LET'S TAKE ANOTHER CALL now. We've got Julie on the line. Hi, Julie."

Mary Anne had switched on the radio as she started her car to drive herself and Cameron to Clare Cureux's house in Myrtle Hollow and obtain a love potion. Hearing the detested voice of her least favorite person, she reached out to turn the radio off again.

"*Don't* touch that dial," Cameron said, batting her hand away.

"Hi, Graham." It was a shy-sounding, young-sounding female voice. "It's about my fiancé."

"You're engaged. Great! That lucky guy."

"The hypocrite," said Mary Anne. "I don't think *he's* ever asked out the same woman twice."

"He's waiting for the real thing," Cameron insisted, undoubtedly partly in jest.

"Thanks," the radio caller said, sounding so sweet that Mary Anne herself listened attentively for her problem, the problem the young woman expected to resolve by listening to *Life—with Dr. Graham Corbett,* which Mary Anne thought of as *Get a Life.* "Well, we've been engaged six months and we're planning to be married at Christmas, and I totally love my fiancé, but he does this little thing that kind of bugs me. He says these things. I know he thinks he's being funny, but he really hurts my feelings. Like I'm a little overweight but I'm not superfat, and I was showing him a wedding dress in a *Brides* magazine, and he asked if it comes in plus sizes."

"Creep," Cameron hissed.

"That's not very nice," Graham remarked, sounding compassionate.

From the man who says I have an ass that's made for radio, Mary Anne reflected. *You sorry piece of work.*

"And I'm an English teacher, but I really want to write short stories, and I sent some in, trying to get published, and he says, 'Those who can, do. Those who can't, teach.'"

"Have you told him how these comments make you feel?"

"Yes. He says I'm oversensitive."

Graham made a thoughtful sound. "Julie, I want you to do something for me. I want you to think about how you feel when he says these things. Then, I'd like you to close your eyes... Got them closed?"

It was the intimate older-brother tone that listeners seemed to love. Knowing how little relation it bore to the real Graham Corbett, Mary Anne found it pretty hard to take.

"Yes," said the girl who was engaged to a jerk.

Beside Mary Anne, Cameron had her eyes closed.

"Just imagine spending the rest of your life with someone who says things that make you feel that way."

The poor girl made a slightly distraught sound. Cameron echoed it.

Mary Anne said, "I can't believe you buy in to his act."

"*Shh!*"

"Now, let's try a different experiment," Graham said. "Imagine how you would feel with someone who loves you so much that he wouldn't dream of saying anything that could hurt your feelings. This is going to be a self-confident guy, so he doesn't need to make himself feel strong by making you feel rotten. He's going to say things like, 'I can just imagine you in that dress. You will look so beautiful. But you're always beautiful to me. I love you so *much*. I cannot *wait* till you're my wife.'"

Mary Anne was not sentimental, but she had to admit that Graham was on the money with this one, and he certainly had a gift for conveying such sentiments in a way that sucked in the female audience.

Beside her, Cameron sighed.

"It's all lies, Cam. That's *not* what he's really like. Trust me."

"*Shh!* This is therapeutic for me. It keeps me from being a godless man-hater."

"Yeah," Julie said softly. "Okay. I see."

"Julie, you don't seem oversensitive to me, but this

clown does seem *under*sensitive. He has some growing up to do, and I'd make sure he does it *before* you get to the altar."

"Amen," Mary Anne said. "Or else you'll end up with someone who says you've got an ass made for radio."

"Who said that?" Cameron asked, eyes suddenly wide and vigilant, turning in her seat.

Mary Anne's cell phone rang. Knowing that up in Myrtle Hollow she might not have reception, she pulled over near the historic Henlawson Bridge and answered. "Mary Anne Drew."

"Hi, Mary Anne, this is Jonathan."

"Jonathan." Why was he calling? She wouldn't be recording her next essay until the following Tuesday. This was Thursday.

"Hey, Angie and I are engaged, and we're having a little party upstairs at the station Saturday night. I wanted to make sure you're there. Angie wants to meet you."

His words jolted her. Thinking she might throw up from the emotional impact of hearing *him* say he was engaged, Mary Anne managed to answer, "Thanks, Jonathan. I'll be there."

"Great. See you then."

She shut the phone, closing her eyes and trying to imagine Jonathan Hale telling *her* that she was always beautiful to him.

Cameron lifted her eyebrows.

Mary Anne repeated what he said.

"A party?" Cameron echoed. "People drink things at parties."

Mary Anne followed her thought and her mischievous

tone to its obvious conclusion. Grimly she put the car in gear, heading for her last hope, for the thing that couldn't possibly work.

Myrtle Hollow

THE HOUSE WAS in fact a cabin. When Mary Anne parked her RAV4 outside, a bearded white-haired man was loading heavy cardboard boxes into a pickup truck. He glanced at the women in the vehicle and she saw a flash of turquoise-blue eyes.

"That's Paul's dad," Cameron said. "He used to be an obstetrician. He lives in your neighborhood."

"David Cureux," Mary Anne replied, thinking with annoyance of the man she knew to be David Cureux's next-door neighbor—Graham Corbett. "City councilman, possibly implicated in the misuse of city funds."

"He absolutely wasn't," Cameron said. "Anyhow, he and Clare are divorced, but they're still good friends. Well—at least he's always helping her with projects. Paul," she pronounced, "has *mother* issues. He needs therapy."

"Of course, he does," Mary Anne retorted. "His mother brews love potions in her spare time."

The woman who came out onto the porch wore her still dark but white-threaded hair in a long braid. The years had etched a map of grooves on her olive-toned skin. The dark eyes seemed only briefly interested in Mary Anne and turned fiercely on the white-haired man, as though supervising him at his task. She wore a flannel shirt and blue jeans, and her feet were bare.

Cameron said, "She never wears shoes unless she's

forced to go somewhere they're required. Paul finds that mortifying, too. Myself, I like her."

"Does she know we're coming?"

"Possibly, but I didn't call her to ask, if that's what you mean."

Uneasily, Mary Anne touched the driver's door handle as Cameron got out of the passenger seat. *What in hell am I doing?*

"David," said the gray-haired woman, "why don't you see if the library can use some of them?"

"The library has no use for thirty-year-old phone books. *You* could have used them for kindling."

Clare seemed to think this over.

He hurried to get behind the wheel, as if afraid she was going to ask him to unload the cardboard boxes he'd just loaded into the truck bed. He shut the door and drove off.

The maker of love potions scowled.

"Waste," she said to Cameron. "People are going to regret all the things they throw out when it all falls apart."

Cameron said, "Hi, Clare. This is Mary Anne Drew. We've come to ask you about—"

"A love potion," Clare answered. "Let's go inside."

Cameron cast Mary Anne a sidelong look, inviting her to be impressed by the woman's powers. Mary Anne wished she was back at the newspaper office, accepting defeat with dignity.

The walls of the cabin's kitchen were lined with shelves full of canning jars containing leaves, roots and other unidentifiable things. Clare asked, "Would either of you like a cup of tea?"

"No, thank you. I'm fine." Mary Anne was a little bit uneasy about accepting a cup of tea from someone who brewed love potions. Whatever this woman made, would it be safe to give Jonathan? What if it poisoned him?

"Thank you," Cameron said. "Do you have nettles?"

"Yes." Clare gave her an approving nod. Mary Anne wondered again why Cameron didn't simply marry Paul, who was handsome, intelligent and employed—a keeper and interpreter at the state park zoo by day and a musician by night. Except that Cameron didn't especially *want* to be married, and she had said Paul definitely didn't want to be and she didn't like him that way anyhow. But Cameron seemed so at home in this atmosphere.

In contrast, Mary Anne felt out-of-place, felt exactly what she was. A woman who liked highlights and pedicures and bikini waxes and shopping and New York, who wouldn't reject the idea of Botox or tooth bleaching, who could lie around watching entire seasons of *Sex and the City* on DVD over and over again.

They sat at a beautiful handmade wooden table on mismatched chairs.

Mary Anne said, "Cameron, this is unnecessary."

Cameron gave her a fierce look.

"Good," said Clare.

Mary Anne blinked. Wasn't this woman peddling snake oil? But she seemed to be encouraging Mary Anne not to buy a love potion.

"Mary Anne," Cameron said, "I think they work."

"They work," Clare agreed. "But usually not in the way people intend."

Despite herself, Mary Anne found her curiosity piqued. But surely Cameron didn't believe—

"What do you mean?" Mary Anne asked Clare.

The woman's gaze was penetrating—a basilisk stare.

"I tell people everything. I give them their instructions for activating the potions. They follow the instructions. Then, unexpected things happen. For instance, you are thinking of giving a love potion to a man who has a girlfriend."

"Actually, they're engaged." The journalist side of Mary Anne was scrupulously truthful. "How did you know that?"

Clare ignored the question. "Yes, well, if he drinks my potion and falls in love with you, things may get messy with the other woman. You need to look into your heart and make sure that this is what you really want, because the person who drinks the potion will fall in love with you with a force you'll be unable to stop or countermand."

"*That* wouldn't be a problem," Mary Anne reflected. "For me, I mean."

Clare gave her an almost disapproving look. "It's better to let nature take its course, you know. You think you know what you want, but it's very important you understand that the experience may be different from what you're expecting."

Mary Anne was quite sure that *all* the ways Jonathan Hale could fall in love with her would be wonderful. She shrugged. The love potion couldn't work, so what was the big deal? "I'll take my chances."

That look again, the expression of a woman who was warning against disaster and knew that the person she warned was deaf to the message. Clare donned reading glasses and opened a spiral notebook, making a notation with a short stub of pencil. She was a thin, reedy woman, not at all bent by age. Drawing a resolute breath, she turned a page in the notebook.

"You'll do it?" Mary Anne said.

"Of course."

The teakettle whistled. Soon a concoction that smelled like grass clippings sat in front of Cameron. "Nettles," Cameron said. "They make your hair grow."

Mary Anne envisioned her cousin with Rapunzel-like tresses—which wasn't too far from what Cameron actually had already.

While Clare worked, mixing various ingredients into a clear liquid, straining, tapping, the journalist in Mary Anne came alive. What went into a love potion? The only ingredient she could identify was a piece of chocolate. Seeing her looking, Clare said, "Green and Black's Organic Extra Dark. Here, have a piece."

Mary Anne took it warily and ate the piece. She had to admit, it was extraordinary chocolate. "It won't hurt him, will it?" she asked. "The love potion?"

Cameron put her head in her hands and shook it.

Clare simply looked at her. "Write this down," she instructed. "Just take a piece of paper out of that notebook. A blank piece, please."

Mary Anne did as directed, picking up the stub of pencil.

"This is what you need to do to activate the potion," Clare said, working with the clear liquid as she spoke. "You must perform three acts of love, each for a person you dislike, someone you can safely say you don't particularly love. It can be one, two or three people. Break it down anyway you like. Just make sure it's someone you quite detest, someone you think is a terrible person."

Graham Corbett leaped to mind.

"You must give one of these people a treasured possession of yours. You must speak to a disliked individual drink. He shoulun ̶ ̶

"Don't you need a piece of my h̶a̶i̶r̶" Mary Anne asked, deciding not to repeat the questio̶n̶ about the potion hurting Jonathan.

The look the midwife gave her was withering. "No, I don't," was all she said. Then, seeing Mary Anne's still doubtful expression, she seemed to take pity and explained, "Your essence is there. Believe me."

Mary Anne tore out the piece of paper. "What do I owe you?" If this was expensive, she was going to kill Cameron.

"Twenty-five dollars."

Cheaper than highlights. Mary Anne readily produced the cash.

Clare stared hard into her eyes and said, "Finally, the most important thing."

"What?"

"Make sure the right person drinks it."

Cameron and Mary Anne both laughed. Mary Anne said, "Won't be a problem."

CHAPTER TWO

A *TREASURED POSSESSION*, a kind word, a secret good deed. Graham Corbett was the obvious recipient of all these things. "A terrible person," Mary Anne murmured with satisfaction as she steered the car out of Myrtle Hollow.

She had forty-eight hours in which to accomplish these tasks. Then, she could slip the potion into a drink for Jonathan at his engagement party. And watch her happiness unfold.

Except that love potions did not work, *could* not work.

Beside her, Cameron said, "I'll come back to Nanna's with you, then walk home."

A good three miles, but nothing for Cameron.

"I can drop you," Mary Anne said.

"No, I want some books."

Aside from a set of the Encyclopedia Britannica, published in 1969, nearly all the books at their grandmother's house, where Mary Anne also lived, were romance novels. No pirates, nothing sexy. Also, nothing published since the early 1950s—Mary Anne suspected that sexy romances had been written before then, but Nanna owned none of them. In Nanna's books, the heroines were constitutionally upbeat virgins who never smoked, drank or kissed on dates, not only because it might be bad for them but also because it might set a bad example for their peers. American heroes and heroines were fiercely patriotic and always punctual. No one ever even mentioned sex. The only historicals Nanna owned had been written by Barbara Cartland—Nanna didn't even particularly care for Jane Austen. Mary Anne believed that this was because Lydia Bennet had lived in sin with wicked Wickham before Darcy had bribed Wickham to marry the ruined creature. Cameron countered that it was because Fitzwilliam Darcy stirred Nanna's own repressed sexual nature. *Pride and Prejudice* was, Cameron maintained, an inherently sexy book.

Both cousins, however, shared an enjoyment of Nanna's selection of extremely unlikely romances. Cameron claimed that in her own case it was historical research into the evils of the repressed society from which all her clients' problems sprang, the seeds planted generations earlier. Mary Anne just enjoyed the stories' improbable plots. "I just finished *Stars in Your Eyes*," she recommended.

Cameron frowned. "Which one is that?"

"The girl is driving to Mexico to take care of her brother's daughter, when she gets a flat tire. A seedy character directs her to a mechanic at the nearest bar, where a total stranger greets her as though they're eloping together. While he's embracing her, he whispers, 'I'm Drex. *Danger.*'"

"And the heroine falls right into the act with him," Cameron said, remembering. "Then, the corrupt Mexican military dude forces them at gunpoint to marry, with the seedy guy presiding as J.P.," she filled in excitedly. "Then, the hero persuades her to keep up the pretense of the marriage—"

"Without ever consummating it—"

"For patriotic reasons involving espionage. Yes, I want that one," Cameron decided. "Do you think Nanna has made us strange? I mean, she made your mother *and* my mother strange."

Mary Anne had little interest in this topic. Her parents lived in Florida and she lived in West Virginia. Another continent might be preferable, but you couldn't have everything. "Do you think the love potion will work?" she asked. "No, I'm stupid. There's no way it can."

"Paul says they *do* work. He says it's scary."

"For someone terrified of commitment, I'm sure it is."

"It's like this, Mary Anne. I work in a job that encourages me to believe romance is silly, marriages don't last and happily ever after is a mundane matter of avoiding men who beat you. But your parents are still married and so are mine."

"Would *you* be in my mother's marriage?" Mary Anne asked.

"No. Nor my own mother's. I'm just trying to say…" Cameron sighed. "I don't know what I'm trying to say. Except that even if the love potion *doesn't* work, you shouldn't stop believing you can have an excellent future with *someone*."

"That's the most depressing thing I ever heard." It was depressing because she wasn't in love with a random *someone*. She wanted Jonathan Hale. "So can you, by the way. Have an excellent future with *someone*."

"It doesn't matter for me. I want to adopt children. I'm not a marriage-or-nothing-else kind of person."

"And I am?"

Cameron said what Mary Anne knew on some level to be true. "Yes."

Mary Anne tried to think of a treasured possession she was willing to sacrifice toward the goal of achieving her heart's desire. What *were* her most treasured possessions? She treasured the quilt Nanna had made for her and given her when she graduated from Columbia. *No way* would that find its way to Graham Corbett's bedroom—a place she pondered only briefly as an imagined horror of dirty underwear and stinky men's running shoes. What else did she treasure?

Cameron said, "So you're going to bestow all these things on Graham Corbett?"

"Yes. I detest him."

"I'm not sure that's the message you'll convey."

Mary Anne heard a slight strain in Cameron's voice. *She really likes him.*

A brainstorm occurred to her. "How's this? For the really nice thing I'm going to do for him?"

Cameron said nothing, just waited.

"I'll set him up with you!"

Cameron muttered something entirely uncharacteristic. "I don't think I'm his type."

"But don't you *want* to go out with him?"

"I want *him* to want to go out with *me*," Cameron corrected.

"He's truly a jerk, dear cousin. You have no idea. He says the most offensive things to me."

"I've heard some of them," Cameron replied, sounding more dejected. "It's called flirting, Mary Anne."

"Oh, no, it's not!" Mary Anne replied. "But if you're game, I can do a thing for him that is far better than he deserves, and set him up with wonderful you."

Cameron shrugged, as if she already knew that Graham would refuse. "Sure."

THE VALUED POSSESSION that Mary Anne decided to sacrifice was Flossy. It was ridiculous for a thirty-two-year-old to be so attached to a stuffed white rabbit with plastic fangs. She'd received it as a twenty-first birthday present from her college boyfriend, and she'd learned afterward that it had been made because of something to do with Monty Python. Her boyfriend had loved Monty Python, but she'd never watched the shows and thought they were stupid. Nonetheless, she'd absolutely fallen in love with Flossy, who her boyfriend had always called "the fluffy little bunny rabbit."

It was going to have to be Flossy. Mary Anne would give it to Graham anonymously. He probably liked Monty Python. She could part with a stuffed animal in the cause of securing the love of Jonathan Hale.

The kind word would be easy. She'd choke down the bile that would inevitably rise to her throat and tell Graham Corbett that his advice to the woman with the mean fiancé had been good. Then she'd set him up with Cameron. What *did* her cousin see in the man?

GRAHAM CORBETT stopped by the radio station at nine the next morning. His plans for the day included working on his book, the first self-help book he'd ever set out to write. He already had a contract with a major publisher; because of the nationwide broadcasts of his radio show, not to mention a few appearances on national television talk shows, his name recognition—and face recognition—had helped to sell this first project, *Life—and Love—with Graham Corbett.*

He had noticed the irony, given that his own love life was thin on the ground. He knew all the reasons that was the case. Briony's death had left him shaken. Not the grief—he had experienced the grief, lived through it. No, it was the way he'd come unraveled, the destruction he'd allowed his emotions to wreak on his life. After a thing like that... Well, he was uneasy about truly binding himself to a woman again.

Uncharacteristically, Mary Anne Drew was at the station when he arrived. He gathered, from her interaction with Jonathan Hale, that she'd just recorded one of her essays. The essays were great. They painted Appalachian life in familiar colors and seemed to always strike an emotional chord. The woman could write and she had a good radio voice, a distinctive alto.

But what did she see in Jonathan Hale? As he stopped near his In basket, Graham could almost feel the longing in Mary Anne...for Hale. She was desperate, no doubt because of the engagement.

Well, whatever.

He stared at his In tray. In it sat a white plush rabbit with vinyl fangs. It was the Killer Rabbit of Caerbannog from *Monty Python and the Holy Grail,* but it wasn't his. He picked it up bemusedly and addressed Mary Anne and Hale, the only other people at the station. "Whose is this? It was in my In tray."

"Then, it must be yours," Hale replied. "Perhaps you have a secret admirer." He chimed in then with a near-perfect imitation of the appropriate section of the movie. Mary Anne laughed, and even her laughter, Graham noticed, seemed desperate.

Graham held the rabbit toward Mary Anne. "Do you know anything about this?"

Her face flushed, but it was probably because Hale had just put his hand on her shoulder and said, "Great essay."

Mary Anne shook her head at Graham.

Graham shrugged and tucked the rabbit under his arm as he collected the other things in his tray. Better not pay too much attention to Mary Anne. She didn't like him, and it bothered him that she had gotten under his skin a bit. Being attached to a woman was something he didn't need. Occasional dates, sure. But the rest…

What had happened after Briony's death still made him ashamed. Drunkenness, failure to appear at appointments or for studio engagements, random couplings with virtual strangers, a sort of unconscious yet full-power course of life destruction. One morning, he had actually awoken naked and hungover on the university athletic field with a broken ankle, like a character from a Tennessee Williams play. And why this descent into debauchery? Because he'd loved her so much? Even after half a year in a grief group and hours of counseling he wasn't sure. He thought it was the shock of death itself. That someone could be there—then gone. His father had passed away a year after Briony, but that had touched him less. His father's life had been a celebration, and it hadn't shocked Graham when an eighty-year-old man slowly dying of asthma had stopped breathing and then become free. Briony's death had been a different situation. A young woman, vibrantly, almost indecently healthy, an athlete, her life so *alive*… Then, gone.

And so he'd had to live to the extent of life, had to live so as to constantly court death.

In any case, now his life was ordered as he liked it, and he wanted to hold on to those things that were most precious—his work, his close relationships, his commitment to all that mattered to him.

Jonathan Hale headed for his office, the only actual office at the station—a small room with a view of Stratton Street. Mary Anne said, "Um, Graham. I wanted to talk to you."

He lifted his eyebrows. Mary Anne *never* voluntarily spoke to him. And maybe that was part of what needled him about her. Not to mention the sheer *waste* of her infatuation with Hale.

He stepped toward her. For all his teasing of her, Graham had to admit that Mary Anne Drew was an extraordinarily good-looking woman. She was tall, strong like an Amazon, with straight Florida surfer-girl hair. She could easily have been a model on the basis of her face. Lush dark eyebrows and eyelashes, green eyes, defined cheekbones and chin, generous mouth, a few freckles on that skin that always looked honey-colored. Yeah, he gave her a hard time about her butt, yet it was only because he knew that was the part of her body she disliked the most. He liked it. You could see her glutes, and she wasn't all skin and bone, like her scrawny cousin.

"I wanted to compliment you on your show yesterday," Mary Anne said.

He lifted an eyebrow.

Her cheeks took on color as he watched.

"Your advice to that girl was so good. It's the kind of thing a lot of women need to hear."

"Thanks," said Graham. This was unprecedented. And a little strange.

"And I wanted to do you a—or ask you for—"

She stumbled around incoherently.

Graham said, "What do you want?"

"I wanted to offer to set you up with Cameron."

"Your cousin," he clarified.

"Yes. She's really nice and she directs the women's resource center, which I'm sure you know. She's had some counseling training, and I thought the two of you might get along."

Graham scratched his head. This was all so strange. "You think I can't get a date?" he asked.

"No." She actually stamped her foot. A small stamp of frustration, but a stamp nonetheless. "I just thought you'd like each other. I thought you could go to Jonathan's party together."

Things were getting more and more weird. "Did she put you up to this?"

"Of course not. Cameron's not like that. She doesn't *need* male attention. She gets plenty of that without help. But she does think you're nice, and I thought the two of you might hit it off."

He squinted. "Cameron... What's her last name?"

"McAllister. Our mothers are sisters. Cameron is really great. I know you'd like her."

Strangely, Mary Anne seemed every bit as desperate in her quest to unite him and her cousin as she was to earn Hale's approval. Graham decided to forgo the "whys." Did he want to go out with Cameron McAllister?

He was selective in choosing dates. He sometimes had trouble getting rid of women after he'd taken them out a few times. One or two had even taken to dropping by the radio station, finding excuses to walk past his house—which wasn't even in town but out in Middleburg, near Mary Anne's grandmother's house. It made him uneasy. He was a public figure. Like it or not, his voice and his radio show, his appearances on television and more, had made him a public figure.

"I really don't know her, Mary Anne," he said. Then, added impulsively, "I have an idea. Why don't I take *you* to Jonathan's party?"

Mary Anne appeared to be considering some serious dilemma in her mind. He could hear the wheels turning and wished he could read her thoughts.

"I—I'd rather you took Cameron," she said.

"And I'd rather take you. Besides—" he lowered his voice, unable to resist "—think of the effect it will have on Hale, seeing us together. For all you know, he might decide you are more of a prize than little Angie." Graham didn't believe this. Hale had no interest in Mary Anne Drew, except as a source of food for his massive ego. Graham simply *had* to tease Mary Anne, whose face grew distinctly red at his words.

She expected him to rise to the bait and spit back at him.

Instead, she said, "Oh, I just don't know," in a way that suggested global warming or world peace might hang on the answer to her inner conflict. She said, again almost desperately, "I'm trying to do something *nice* for you!"

"So go out with me."

"I don't like you!" she replied. "Cameron does. Why don't you go out with her?"

Her behavior was incomprehensible. Graham pushed aside the little sting of that "I don't like you!" He said, "Well, you tried. But to be perfectly honest, it reminds me of the Christmas when I wanted a red ten-speed Bianchi bike and found a five-speed Schwinn under the tree."

She made a startled little noise that might have been the word *Oh,* and looked crestfallen.

He said, "I'll tell you what. You bring Cameron to the party, and we'll see what happens. I've never really talked with her. All I know is she broke Carl Moosegow's wrist."

"He grabbed her in a bar!" Mary Anne exclaimed. "And not on the arm, either. She's studied martial arts. It was a case of 'no mind,' like Bruce Lee used to talk about. She just reacted as she'd been trained to do."

"I'll be careful where my hands stray," said Graham, who had counseled female clients on maintaining boundaries—and dealing with men who did not observe them. "By the way, are *you* trained in martial arts?"

Without a word, she spun away, grabbed her purse and left the office.

Graham grinned as he watched her go…and exchanged a look with the Killer Rabbit of Caerbannog, who grinned right back.

HE HADN'T LET HER do something nice for him, and Mary Anne was unsure whether "It's the thought that counts" applied to good deeds required to activate love potions. A simple solution would have been to agree to go to the party with him, but Mary Anne didn't like him, so how could that have been doing him a good deed? She *couldn't* have gone with him, though. Because of Cameron. Cameron liked him, and Mary Anne didn't want to hurt Cameron.

Objecting to the idea of putting more effort into the love potion project, yet unwilling to simply abandon it, she took a gift certificate for Pizza Hut pizza that she'd won at the high school's kickoff carnival and slipped it into Graham's In tray. After that, the only thing to do was mildly discourage Cameron's interest in Graham, play down any possibility that Graham actually liked Mary Anne herself and prepare to slip Jonathan Hale a love potion.

"DO I LOOK OKAY?" she asked Cameron on the night of the engagement party. "Do these jeans make my butt look big?"

"You have an excellent butt," Cameron replied matter-of-factly. Blessed with a figure that Mary Anne, for one, believed was the answer to every man's fantasies, Cameron had absolutely no interest in discussing Mary Anne's figure flaws. "And your clothes are cool. You look like a model."

Low-rise flare jeans, baby T-shirt and her favorite hat. She also wore her favorite moss-green wrap sweater coat.

In her handbag was the precious vial she'd bought from Clare Cureux.

Tonight was the night.

Taking her turn in front of the mirror, Cameron babbled, "Jonathan asked Paul to play for the party but I told Paul he couldn't, because if he's there I have to pretend we're together."

It was a situation Mary Anne still couldn't get her head around, but all she said was, "And so he turned down the gig?"

"Oh, sure. That's not usually part of our agreement, but he knows how badly I want to go out with Graham." After a moment, she said, "Besides, he knew he could get a different gig tonight. He just told Jonathan he was booked, and then he got a gig—so he was." She changed the subject. "Do I look okay?"

Mary Anne scrutinized her cousin. Cameron was dressed up, for her. She wore a low-backed brown dress and clunky platform shoes. She looked sexy and great and had probably spent a total of six dollars on the ensemble. "You're an eleven," Mary Anne told her, blowing her a kiss. "He's lucky you're coming, but you'll get to see for yourself what he's really like."

Cameron gave a mischievous grin that showed her chipped front tooth, an anomaly in her otherwise perfect bite. "Graham Corbett, here I come!"

Mary Anne decided that if Graham tried to flirt with *her* tonight instead of her cousin, she would pour a drink on him.

THE PARTY TOOK PLACE in the Embassy Ballroom, which occupied the entire floor above the radio station in the Embassy Building. Mary Anne had learned that the landlord was letting the engaged couple use it as a gift to Jonathan Hale, a tribute for his work for WLGN.

Before they headed upstairs, Mary Anne said, "Want to use the ladies' room?"

"Sure."

Mary Anne opened the radio station's glass door. The recording booth was occupied by two indie kids prerecording a music program. She gave them a wave as she and Cameron headed past the rows of desks and computers to the restrooms.

"There's Flossy!"

"Yes." Mary Anne didn't even steal a glance at the desk Graham claimed as his at the station—or the white rabbit sitting on top of it. "Let's not talk about it." Cameron, of course, was privy to the steps Mary Anne had taken to activate the love potion. Well, except all the details of her failure to set him up with Cameron. She'd confessed to her cousin only that the Pizza Hut gift certificate had been "simpler."

Cameron remarked, "If you didn't hate him so much, I'd think you liked him." She wasn't talking about Flossy, now.

"Ha-ha," said Mary Anne, without interest or humor as she marched into the ladies' room.

Angie Workman stood alone before the sinks, leaning forward on tiptoe in her stiletto heels to apply red lipstick to her wide mouth. "Oh, hi. It's Mary Anne, right?"

Besides being impossibly tiny, with a figure to die for, Angie had wonderful hair. It was very thick, very curly and platinum-blond…true blond. In contrast, her eyebrows and eyelashes were so dark they looked fake. Regrettably, she held her hair back with barrettes in a style that showed zero imagination. Her dress was a synthetic blend, white with autumn leaves, and her stilettos were also white. A part of Mary Anne, which she acknowledged as mean-spirited and extremely jealous, thought, *Hello, it's October! You don't wear white shoes in October.*

If Angie knew nothing about fashion, the fact had obviously made no impact on Jonathan Hale. With a lurch of her heart, Mary Anne saw the diamond on Angie's delicate left hand.

Mary Anne held out her own hand. "Yes, and you're Angie. It's nice to meet you. This is Cameron McAllister."

"I so admire your radio essays," Angie told Mary Anne with obvious sincerity. "I wish I could write something like the things you say. I listen to you every week. My favorite one was the one about the Civil War cemetery—about the brothers who fought on different sides of the conflict."

"Thank you." Mary Anne's emotions were mixed. She felt proud and happy because of Angie's words. And yet she planned to steal Angie's fiancé. She could tell that Angie was obviously a nice person, one of those deeply genteel people that the West Virginia mountains sometimes produced. A twinge of shame ran through Mary Anne, and she remembered Clare Cureux's warnings. How would Jonathan's falling in love with Mary Anne impact Angie? What if being jilted was the kind of thing Angie couldn't get over?

Now Angie turned to Cameron. "And everyone says such good things about your work at the women's center. My friend Rhonda says you're an angel to those women."

All delivered in a West Virginia twang that seemed the pinnacle of charm.

Cameron smiled politely. As Jonathan's fiancée excused herself to return to the party, Cameron glanced at Mary Anne.

"I know," Mary Anne said. "She's sweet and adorable."

Cameron said, "Maybe. But I'm not an angel."

JONATHAN WAS DRINKING a Frog's Leap cabernet. Mary Anne discovered this in a brief moment of conversation with him as she sipped her own merlot. She managed to tell him how nice she thought Angie was and ask what he thought of her idea for next week's essay—October celebrations—all while watching the level of wine in his wineglass and praying for a moment of opportunity.

Jonathan, however, was engaged in a distracted conversation with one of the female disc jockeys who was also the friend and future bridesmaid of Angie Workman. Her name was Elinor Sweet.

Jonathan said, "What color dress you wear is between you and Angie. I couldn't care less."

"But you could intervene. I mean, orange? Me, in orange?"

Elinor had honey-toned skin, which would probably look great in anything.

Jonathan looked over at Graham and said, "Graham, please explain to Elinor why it would be a mistake for me to try to choose the color of the bridesmaids' dresses."

Mary Anne watched Graham Corbett and Cameron join the group.

Cameron said, "I'm sure Angie would want to know how you feel about wearing orange, Elinor. If it were *my* wedding, I would want to know."

Mary Anne met Cameron's eyes briefly and knew her cousin was dying to add, *And you wouldn't be in it.*

Graham said, "I think etiquette dictates that the bride's wishes carry the day."

"But who wants a wedding color that will look bad on bridesmaids?" Mary Anne asked. "Tell Angie how you feel, Elinor. Though I'm sure anything would look great on you."

"But the question is," Jonathan said, "if I should step in. Obviously, I shouldn't."

"Obviously," Graham echoed.

Mary Anne wanted to scream that *obviously* the bride should choose colors and clothes that would look good on her friends, and whoever heard of bridesmaids dressed in orange? She asked Graham, "What makes you the expert on weddings?"

"He's the WLGN relationship expert," Jonathan said.

Mary Anne rolled her eyes. "A *man.*"

"What's wrong with men?" Graham asked.

"It's just a bit one-sided. That's all."

Jonathan's eyes lit up, as if what she'd said had struck home with him. "That gives me an idea…" He glanced at his nearly empty glass.

Mary Anne was vigilant.

As he took the last sip, she drained half of her own glass in one long gulp and lifted Jonathan's glass airily from his hand. "Another for you, groom-to-be?"

Distracted, he glanced at her. "Oh. Thank you, Mary Anne. When you come back—"

But she was already walking away, leaving the crowd behind.

This was the moment. She carried both glasses to the refreshment table, which was unattended. She found the cabernet and carefully poured another glass, holding the uncapped vial of potion against her palm, and letting it run into his glass with the wine.

It couldn't work, but what the hell?

Frowning slightly, she spotted Angie again. Far from spending every moment on her fiancé's arm, Angie was speaking intently to Max Harold, the Embassy Building's custodian. Max used to work in the mines and could talk for hours. Mary Anne had to admit the old man was interesting, but clearly Angie was a good listener.

There was, Mary Anne told herself, nothing *wrong* with what she planned to do. All was fair in love and war.

She poured herself another glass of merlot and took a sip to steady her nerves.

"Ah, thank you, Mary Anne."

A masculine hand took Jonathan's glass from her hand.

Mary Anne did not release it. "No, that's for—" She could *not* let the glass go.

Appalled, she felt the stem break, the base coming off in her hand.

Graham Corbett looked in astonishment from the piece she held to the glass he held.

She reached for his part of the glass just as he lifted it to his lips and drank deeply.

Mary Anne could not breathe. Her mouth was open, she was half-panting, her hand still reaching, reaching…

"Excellent," Graham said and gazed at her thoughtfully.

She wanted to swear.

But she couldn't even breathe. Everything was swimming. Her head was swimming. And the glass was empty.

CHAPTER THREE

MARY ANNE STUMBLED into Graham, and he caught her.

She smelled earthy, sexy and natural. He studied the scattering of freckles across her nose, the paintbrush lashes, the full lips.

"Are you all right?" he asked.

Mary Anne sank onto a folding chair near the table. "Yes. Yes."

"What happened?" Jonathan Hale joined them, gazing in concern at her.

Graham saw that earlier expression of horror wisp over her face again.

Mary Anne pushed herself out of the chair. "Nothing happened. I'm fine. Just a bit light-headed."

"You're a skinny thing," Jonathan told her. "If you haven't eaten, let's get something in you."

Graham felt irrational annoyance. "She's not fading away."

Her part of the glass had rolled away on the floor, and Jonathan picked it up. Graham handed the other part to him and focused on Mary Anne. She was a strong, healthy woman, vibrant as a Thoroughbred horse. This one was no fading lily or shrinking violet or whatever it was that was supposed to be prized in Southern women, and he didn't believe she was light-headed, either. *Probably just upset about Hale and Miss Workman.* He looked at Jonathan, who was handing her a bottle of water.

"Thanks," she said, taking it gratefully, uncapping it and then simply gazing at the bottle, looking shattered.

Jonathan put a hand on her back, and she gave him a look that seemed to say, *What in the hell are you doing touching me?*

In fact, Mary Anne was now wondering if she'd actually seen Graham Corbett drink the glass of wine she'd spiked with love potion. And if she had seen that, as she was sure she had, why was Jonathan Hale suddenly noticing her existence? She whispered, "I need to... I need to go home."

"You can't drive," Jonathan said. "Just sit down, and let's get you something to eat. You've been manhandled."

"What?" Graham said in disbelief.

"You were fighting with her over *my* glass of wine," Jonathan replied.

"Didn't know it was yours, but I did not *manhandle* Mary Anne."

Jonathan ignored Graham. "I'll get myself another," he told Mary Anne gently. "Thanks for trying."

"Ah, Cameron." Graham turned to Mary Anne's cousin and dropped some keys into her hand. "My car's just outside in the bank parking lot. Why don't you take it and meet us at Mary Anne's house? Can you drive a shift? I'll drive Mary Anne in her car."

"Maybe we should hear what Mary Anne wants," Jonathan said, staring intently at Graham.

And they all, Graham and Jonathan and Cameron, looked at Mary Anne, as if to discover what she wanted.

She had no answer, except that Graham was paying attention to her in front of Cameron, who couldn't help seeing the direction of the wind. And Jonathan was finally noticing her—but he was engaged! Everything was messed up and she wished she'd never gotten involved with the love potion that Graham Corbett had drunk.

She stared at the bottle of water and lifted it to her mouth, drinking deeply. Drinking in a clear, bright thought.

Love potions don't work anyhow.

MARY ANNE MADE her excuses—to Jonathan and his fiancée and to Cameron, who *had* secured the promise of a ride home from Graham—and was back at her grandmother's house before ten, just as Nanna's housekeeper and attendant, Lucille, was about to turn out Jacqueline Billingham's bedroom light. Putting the debacle with the love-potion-that-wouldn't-work-anyway behind her, Mary Anne hurried upstairs to kiss her grandmother good-night.

Nanna still sat up against a three-cornered pillow, wearing a nightgown made of some delicate cotton that reminded Mary Anne of the woman's soft skin, grown thinner with age yet always seeming smooth and young. As usual, her grandmother smelled good, the scent of her night cream reminding her of roses. An Emilie Loring novel, marked with a lace bookmark, sat on the bedside table next to Nanna's water glass and rosary beads. Mary Anne kissed her, and Nanna, her white hair loose for the night, asked, "Did you have a good time, dear?"

"Yes," Mary Anne lied blithely.

"And did Cameron come back with you?"

"No," Mary Anne said. "She has a ride home with

someone else." Mary Anne steered the conversation carefully away from mentioning any possibility of Cameron
being, in any sense, *with* a man. Rationally, she knew this
was unnecessary. However, some genetic reflex compelled her to participate in the family conspiracy of pretending the world was like one of Nanna's romance
novels. Even if sometimes it seemed to her that the
pretense was subsuming her own reality.

Mary Anne had been a rebellious teenager, a Florida
surfer girl. Every summer, her mother had sent her north
to Logan, where Mary Anne, rather than succumbing to
her grandmother's influence, had spent every free
moment with Cameron and the sort of boys their mothers
hated, doing every forbidden thing one could arrange
and usually escaping detection.

After that, Mary Anne had gone away to university in
New York City, but she'd still returned to Logan each
summer. Gradually, she had ceased to be a hellion, had
entered therapy to help her accept everything she hated
about her family and had become a decent contract bridge
player, who could prepare a nice-looking dish for a
church potluck and who sent thank-you notes on time.

It was now five years since Mary Anne had come to
live with Nanna. The drawback was that Mary Anne
could not bring a man to her grandmother's house for the
night or allow her grandmother to know that she would
spend the night at a man's house. Her grandmother did
not want the world to be the kind of place where men and
women who were not married to each other had sexual
intercourse. So Mary Anne was due an Oscar for lifetime
achievement, for pretending she would never consider
sleeping with a man outside of marriage. The most dif-

ficult part of the pretense was that Mary Anne simply couldn't lie to her grandmother.

So for five years she hadn't spent the night with a man.

She'd had rare, brief sexual encounters with men at their homes and then said she needed to get home, citing newspaper deadlines. Because the world could not wait for her feature on the Logan Garden Tour.

Cameron had once asked her, "What's Nanna going to do if you ever want to move in with someone? A man, I mean."

"There's no one I want to move in with," Mary Anne had replied. "Anyhow, the same applies to you."

"No, it doesn't. Nanna knows I've lived with men."

This was true. Nanna had simply said, "Oh, my," and, "Darling, could you find this color of embroidery floss in my bag? My eyes are having trouble picking it out."

Mary Anne wasn't sure what she thought would happen if *she* let Nanna down by doing what Cameron had done with so little consequence. Nonetheless, she couldn't bring herself to disillusion the older woman.

Well, it wasn't going to be a problem anytime soon, Mary Anne reflected later that night as she curled up in her four-poster missing Flossy.

The wrong person had drunk the love-potion-that-would-not-work.

GRAHAM CORBETT LAY on a comfortable, if ugly couch in the master bedroom of his home, his feet on a tile-topped Craftsman encyclopedia table that had been a gift from his mother. The graceful two-story white house, with its wraparound porches and its upper balconies, was too big for one person. Nonetheless, he liked it.

Like Mary Anne Drew, he lived on the exclusive island of old homes known as Middleburg. Reached by a bridge that crossed the river, Middleburg was a charming spot. The hills rose behind his home, sometimes bringing nature closer than he wanted. For instance, there'd been a time last summer when he'd found an eight-foot-long black snake curled up under the swing on his back porch. Graham was not a snake lover and he really didn't give a damn about the inroads they made on the rodent population. He'd headed to the garden shed, intending to grab a shovel and cut off the thing's head, and there he had found a copperhead curled up in his watering can.

He'd gone back to the house and poured himself a whiskey. When he'd returned to the porch, the black snake was gone. He'd knocked back the glass of whiskey and considered what to do about the copperhead in the watering can. First, he must cover the opening in the top of the can so that the snake would not escape. Then, he needed to kill or dispose of the snake. But how?

He was on his second whiskey when his neighbor David Cureux popped over to invite Graham to join a committee to discuss health plans for city workers. Cureux, a former obstetrician, was a council member and had become a friend.

Graham told David about the copperhead. David went home for his shotgun, came back and killed the copperhead. To Graham's astonishment, however, David first dumped the copperhead out of the watering can—explaining that he didn't want to get holes in the can.

Two other neighbors, attracted by the sound of the shotgun, came over to see what was going on. One told

Graham a story about a child carrying baby copperheads in a jar, thinking they were worms, holding his hand over the top of the jar, being bitten repeatedly and then dying from the venom. Subsequently, according to the neighbor, a policeman put the jar of copperheads in the trunk of his car, which then had to be impounded and fumigated to kill the reptiles. David Cureux challenged this story as nonsense, but for weeks Graham dreamed of finding snakes in his automobile, in his bed, in his bathtub, in his basement—virtually everywhere. The woman who recorded the astrology show at the radio station told him that dreams about snakes reflected the evolutionary ability to change, the urge to survive and how he dealt with the impulses of the most ancient part of his brain.

Jonathan Hale had argued that snakes in dreams were definitely about sex.

The astrologer had retorted, "Isn't that what I said?"

Graham thought the dreams were about the basic terror of sitting down on the porch swing and discovering a black serpent of notoriously aggressive nature coiled beside his feet.

Hale. What had the station manager been doing getting touchy-feely with Mary Anne tonight? Wasn't the man supposed to be celebrating his engagement?

Graham needed to stop thinking about the woman. What was this sudden obsession with her? He'd always found her attractive, yes, and he took great pleasure in baiting her, simply because of her worship of Jonathan Hale and her awe of his experiences in Rwanda and Afghanistan. But Graham wasn't sure he wanted a relationship, and in any case Mary Anne had made it clear she wanted nothing to do with him.

Until the strange business of her trying to set him up with Cameron.

Cameron. Cameron did nothing for Graham. She was pretty, if you liked the type. But he thought she was hard, as well. It was her cousin who interested him.

Strange. She'd annoyed him at their very first meeting five years earlier. The former station manager had introduced him to Mary Anne as "a psychologist who hosts a talk show dealing with relationship problems." It hadn't been as slickly phrased as Jonathan Hale would have put it…and did express it after he replaced the former manager. But essentially it had been accurate.

The new kid on the block, fresh from her New York job covering Milan fashion shows or whatever the hell it was she had done, had said, "No doubt calling up a wealth of life experience. It's a pleasure to meet you, Graham. I've heard your show."

Innocuous enough.

But what had she meant about life experience? Puzzled, he'd stopped her at the water cooler a few minutes later and asked her what she meant.

Then, she'd dissembled. She'd shrugged and said, "I mean, we all work with what we've experienced. That's all I meant." And she'd turned away fast. Escaping.

She'd been nasty, and when challenged she'd denied having said anything offensive. Nor was the undercurrent of her words imaginary. Because a week later, she had introduced him to another woman as "the bachelor guru of female satisfaction."

The *bachelor* guru.

Which was inaccurate and incomplete.

Graham Corbett was a widower.

THE PHONE AWOKE Mary Anne the next morning. She saw the numbers on her alarm clock—nine-thirty—and snatched the receiver from its cradle. How had she slept so long? "Hello?"

"Mary Anne? It's Jonathan."

Her heart pounded. "Oh, hi," she said, squinting against the autumn's morning light.

"I just wanted to see how you are this morning. Did you get home okay?"

"Oh. Of course. Thank you. It's really nice of you to check. I was fine. I *am* fine," she corrected.

"Good," he said. "Good."

He sounded as nervous as Mary Anne felt.

He said, "There's something I want to ask you. I ran it by Graham last night, and he was game."

Dark presentiment hovered.

"I heard what you said about him offering a one-sided view on relationships. So I suggested that you be his guest for a four-week segment on dating. If it works out, we could have you there regularly as a guest."

Mary Anne blinked. *Be on Graham Corbett's hideous, tacky talk show?*

But it was exposure. It was something else for her resumé. She wouldn't become a celebrity. It wasn't any different, really, from her radio essays.

But it wasn't as anonymous as journalism. In journalism there was a dignity lacking in—well… She separated herself mentally from her father's public and private personas, which were essentially the same. She would never become like him.

"I'm hardly qualified," she said.

"You're an attractive woman. You date, right?" Jonathan asked.

You're an attractive woman. If only it didn't feel so much as if he was damning her with faint praise. "I date," she confirmed. Occasionally. Almost never lately, because there was no one she wanted *to* date.

"You can do it," Jonathan said. "You'll give great advice."

Like how to steal someone's fiancé with a love potion? The thought of what she'd done the night before was mortifying. In a way, she supposed, it was better that Graham had drunk it. It wasn't going to work, and this way it was as if she hadn't actually tried to spike Jonathan's drink.

Mary Anne said, "I'd like to…think about it."

"Well, I plan to be at the studio most of the day doing paperwork," he said. "Come by if you want to talk about it—or just hang out."

Mary Anne widened her eyes. It was nothing. He was just being a friend. "I…might," she said.

"Great. I'll look for you. We'll go have coffee."

"I said I *might*," she clarified.

"Then, I'll hope," he replied.

She hung up the phone, squinting, heart beating hard, playing the conversation through her mind. *Come by if you want to talk about it—or just hang out.*

Did it mean anything? Was he finally interested in her?

Interested or not, he *was* engaged to another woman.

And he hadn't called her on the phone to say that relationship was broken because he'd suddenly realized he didn't want to marry Angie Workman. Instead, he'd called her and told her he'd be spending the day at the studio. Sunday, when the studio was usually quiet, the station running prerecorded programs.

No, she was being silly. People popped in and out on Sundays.

What if she made an excuse to go down to the station? Was that what he hoped would happen? She couldn't decide whether that was good or bad.

She called Cameron.

"GRAHAM DRANK the love potion."

Cameron's heart sank. It wasn't that she believed the love potion would work. All the same, Graham Corbett's drinking it seemed a sign—a sign that he and Mary Anne were going to end up together.

In any case, he was not attracted to Cameron. If he had been, she would have felt it. *Lots* of men *were* attracted to her. But last night, when Graham had taken her home, he'd seemed deeply preoccupied.

Cameron lived in an old miner's company house that had been moved from its original location to the foot of Jack Hollow. When she'd climbed out of Graham's car, the dogs came to greet her. Wolfie was feral, a black animal almost certainly part wolf, who'd gradually become tame and was loved by the people of the hollow, and his daughter, Mariah, Cameron's own dog. Cameron had glanced into the car at Graham but he was simply waiting, engine idling. No hope.

She told Mary Anne, "I don't think he needed to."

"Needed to do what?"

"Drink the love potion. I think he's already seriously smitten with you."

"Well, I'm not smitten with him. What happened when he took you home?"

"Absolutely nothing."

Mary Anne said, "Well, forget him. *Jonathan* called."

Cameron listened to the details, saying, "But he didn't drink the love potion. Maybe *this* is what Clare meant— that they don't always work the way you think."

"She told me to make sure the right person drinks it."

Cameron considered, curious. "If I'm up at her place again, I'm going to ask her about other things that have happened with love potions." *Maybe she has something that will help me get over my stupid crush on a man who likes my cousin.* "You're going to do the show with Graham, aren't you?"

"I don't know. I'm thinking about it."

Cameron remembered something she'd meant to ask the night before. "Hey, can you help me with Women of Strength next weekend?"

"As long as it's not caving."

Cameron smiled, remembering that on a previous caving trip Mary Anne, who wasn't proportioned for the sport, had gotten stuck in a narrow passage. "It isn't *this* time, but we're doing Big Jim's Cave at the end of November and I want you to do that with us. You *won't* get stuck there."

"What's next week's joy?"

"Hiking and studying wild plants with a local herbalist."

"Sure."

"Good. Okay. I'll talk to you later." The local herbalist was Clare Cureux and Cameron supposed she had some ulterior motive—that perhaps Clare could *remove* Graham's infatuation with Mary Anne. Then, she blinked, feeling sad, knowing that love potions, like happily ever afters, were just dreams from Nanna's books.

CHAPTER FOUR

OCTOBER CELEBRATIONS. October celebrations. October celebrations.

Mary Anne could not focus on the topic she'd chosen for this week's radio essay. It was Monday, and she always went on the air Tuesday afternoons at three-fifty, right before *All Things Considered.*

At two-thirty in the afternoon, she sat in her grandmother's living room playing bridge with Nanna and the Morrisseys, who lived next door. She was struggling to concentrate on the game, knowing only that her essay was not done, had no fire, was nothing.

Nanna had dressed in black slacks and a white blouse. Her hair was straight and white and fell below her shoulders, and she held it back with a black velvet bow clip. She wore her gold hoop earrings. She had a law degree and had clerked in a law office before she met her husband. She was formidable.

Relieved to find herself dummy in the last hand, Mary Anne sat thinking about the fact that she had been so desperately in love with someone that she had spiked his drink with a love potion, which the person she most disliked had seized and drunk. The fact that she'd attempted something so foolish, not to mention childish, as a love potion alarmed her.

"Well," said Nanna, "here we are." Totals, smiles, the rubber, the game. She and Nanna had won.

Mary Anne made polite responses as Mr. Morrissey folded up the card table and as Mrs. Morrissey complimented Nanna on the lemon cake Lucille had made. Finally, the two of them were gone, and Mary Anne told her grandmother, "I better work on my essay. I keep putting it off."

"What's your topic?"

"October celebrations," Mary Anne said with a sigh. "I should probably switch, because it's doing nothing for me."

"Maybe you should look at my community calendar and see what's happening this month." Nanna reached to the table beside her for the small calendar with its photographs of Logan. She flipped it slowly to October, squinted, then handed it to Mary Anne.

Mary Anne looked at the various announcements, reminders and historical anniversaries. Today marked the hundredth anniversary of Logan's first hospital birth. She blinked, thinking of Clare Cureux, a midwife who attended births in homes. And wasn't Clare's ex-husband, David Cureux, an obstetrician—or hadn't he been in the past?

Mary Anne wasn't sure why she felt drawn to the Cureux family, except that she wanted to cover up that first impression she'd made—as a love-potion customer. She wanted them to know that she was a rational person who'd tried the potion just for a lark, just for the sheer goofy fun of it. As if any minute of the experience had been fun.

The other option was to avoid them, to skulk when she passed her neighbor David Cureux's house and try to pretend it had never happened.

No, she wanted to restore her reputation and she wanted to start at the place where she'd begun to destroy it.

"Nanna," she told her grandmother, "you're a genius. This is the anniversary of Logan's first hospital birth, and I'm going to write about birth in Logan County." She studied her grandmother. "Were you born in the hospital?"

"Oh, yes," said Nanna. "And I love your idea." She lifted her face, and Mary Anne kissed the soft skin, taking in the familiar scent of her grandmother's face cream.

"Love you," Mary Anne said.

Lucille stepped into the living room. "Mrs. Billingham, are you ready to go upstairs for a nap?"

"I think so, Lucille."

"Miss Mary Anne," said Lucille, "if you go out, you wrap up good. It's chilly out."

"Thank you, Lucille."

When Mary Anne had first visited her grandmother in West Virginia she'd been a little startled by the tall, elegant black woman who called Nanna "Mrs. Billingham" and called Mary Anne "Miss Mary Anne." It all seemed so *Gone with the Wind*—and just a little bit disturbing. However, she had since come to know Lucille well and had visited her family in nearby Holden and met her son, who was a Porsche mechanic. She'd never succeeded in persuading Lucille to drop the "Miss" in front of her name.

Far be it from Nanna to suggest that Lucille call her "Jacqueline."

Mary Anne went upstairs to collect her car keys, purse and notebook. Her first stop wouldn't require her to drive, however. David Cureux lived right around the corner.

UNFORTUNATELY, when Mary Anne reached the next block, she discovered that he and Graham Corbett were enjoying an afternoon cocktail together on Graham's wide front veranda. *Damn*.

David Cureux must know that the purpose of her visit to his ex-wife had been to obtain a love potion. What if he told Graham? She started to turn, hoping to escape without being seen and bringing the unhappy event to mind, but Graham called out, "Mary Anne!"

Into the fray. Surely, David Cureux wouldn't mention the damn love potion. And if he did, Mary Anne would simply deny it. Maybe she'd say it was for Cameron—it had been Cameron's idea, after all.

"Hi, Graham," she replied. She hadn't discussed Jonathan's proposal for the show with him yet. Maybe that was what he wanted to talk about. But as she climbed the steps to the veranda, she said, "Dr. Cureux, you're the one I was hoping to find. I'm writing an essay on childbirth in Logan County, in celebration of the hundredth anniversary of our first hospital birth."

"Well, now that's an interesting topic," the obstetrician replied, his blue eyes instantly alight.

It would be all right, Mary Anne decided. This was a sensible man, and he probably thought the love potions were nonsense anyhow. *Just as I do.*

"What tack are you going to take on this essay?" he asked.

"Well, it seems obvious to me to talk about hospital births and home births and discuss the fact that both still occur in Logan County. But what usually happens when I write an essay is that I don't know what I'm going to say until I've gathered some stories and mulled the topic over. This idea came to me literally fifteen minutes ago." She knew that as the interviewer, the burden was on her.

"For instance, maybe an interesting place to start would be with the births of your own children. You were married to a midwife who attended births at home."

"Yes, and I would have had to sedate Clare to get her inside a hospital, where she was convinced that terrible things would happen to her. Her births were trouble free, and I attended them."

"Have you attended any other home births in Logan County?"

"Well, a few, and a couple emergencies, too. I delivered a baby during a big rock concert in the seventies—*at* the concert, no less."

Graham watched Mary Anne sit down automatically in the chair he offered. She murmured her thanks without a glance in his direction. She was entirely focused on her interview, which gave him a chance to study her. He'd agreed to Hale's idea, doubting if Mary Anne would do it. She had some bizarre ideas about what was appropriate for a journalist.

David Cureux said, "How are your folks, by the way? I was watching a rerun of one of your dad's movies the other night."

Graham blinked. "Who's your dad, Mary Anne?"

"Jon Clive Drew," David replied.

"No kidding!" Graham exclaimed.

Mary Anne nodded almost impatiently and turned the topic back to childbirth, asking the doctor about his first experience attending a birth at the hospital.

Graham examined her face, looking for a resemblance to the actor who had first become well-known for his role on a daytime soap opera. Jon Clive Drew had moved on from there to portraying villains and heroes in detective dramas, and then he'd hit the big screen where he'd made it very big for a very short time. As Graham recalled, he'd also done some kind of car racing, and he'd recorded some albums, too—folk music, Graham thought. The man had made his mark, though not with his art as much as through his personal life. Graham recalled a photo he'd seen somewhere of Jon Clive at a Miami Beach party, women drawing on his bare chest with lipstick while he grinned in a carefree, dissolute way. How old had Mary Anne been when that had happened? Graham wasn't sure how old he'd been. He also remembered an epic drunken car chase across several states, which had ended when Jon Clive drove off a Texas pier, leaping from the car as it hurtled toward the water. And there was some bar he set on fire after he was insulted at a concert. And affairs with various actresses, one after another. All of these things were always topped off with Jon Clive's public and religious remorse and apologies. Because part of the actor's personality was that he loved to stand by his religion, wanted everyone to know he was a God-fearing man. Yes, Jon Clive had been a professional bad boy. *Had* been, as in has-been. Clearly, Mary Anne didn't find him a worthy topic of conversation.

But Graham couldn't help asking, "And he was on that show...*Miami!*"

"Right." Mary Anne stood up, having nothing more to say about nighttime television's short-lived answer to *Dallas*. "Thank you, Dr. Cureux. You've given me some good things to think about."

"Don't run off," said Graham, standing up as well. "I didn't offer you a drink. I'm sorry."

"No, thanks. I have other things to look into."

Graham said, "About the show—"

"Yes?"

"I'm game if you are," he continued, surprising himself by hoping she wanted to do it.

Mary Anne's lush eyebrows drew together slightly. "All right," she agreed. And with a nod, she left them, hurrying down the steps.

As she left, Graham admired the image her body presented from behind. She was tall and strong, and he liked that about her, liked her straight hair shining like wheat in the sun.

Dr. Cureux regarded him curiously, glanced at the departing woman and then looked back at Graham. "What's this about a show? Your show?"

"She's going to be on it to offer dating advice."

Surprisingly, the physician snorted.

Graham blinked at him, startled. "What?"

David Cureux shook his head and rose wearily from his chair. "I will leave you to go back to your writing, Graham. Thank you for the refreshment."

"You're welcome," Graham replied, wondering if his neighbor knew something about Mary Anne that he didn't know.

Myrtle Hollow

MARY ANNE ONLY wanted to see Clare Cureux again to emphasize that, well, she wasn't the kind of woman who bought love potions or used them. She wanted to show Clare Cureux the *real* Mary Anne Drew. But as she parked by the cabin alongside two other vehicles that hadn't been there the first time she visited, she considered turning around and driving away. She could write her essay without speaking to Clare Cureux.

And what if the woman mentioned the love potion in front of the other people who were inside?

Briefly, Mary Anne studied the cars. One was an ancient navy-blue Volvo station wagon bearing two bumper stickers, one supporting the Logan County Women's Resource Center and the other suggesting that none of the current candidates for president was conservative enough.

He put it on there to annoy his mother, Cameron had said. *See what I mean about mother issues?*

Okay, so that was Paul Cureux's car. Mary Anne had met him, through Cameron, with whom he seemed like a bad older brother who lured his sister into stunts that would get them both into trouble. The other vehicle contained two children's car seats and an assortment of pro-children, pro-home birth, anti-immunization, pro-vegetarian bumper stickers.

Mary Anne placed the car with a face. The dreadlock woman. Oh, good grief—Clare Cureux's hippie daughter, Bridget—Paul's actual sister. Mary Anne couldn't help wondering if *her* bumper stickers had been chosen in part to annoy her father.

She was thinking of backing out again, driving away, escaping, when Clare, herself, appeared on the porch.

Too late to flee now.

Mary Anne got out, dragging purse and notebook after her and speaking before she even reached the porch. "Hi, I hope it's not a bad time. I'm writing an essay on a hundred years of birth in Logan County."

Clare said, "The wrong person drank it, didn't he?"

How had she known? Only Cameron knew... Telegraph, telephone or "tell Cameron," Mary Anne thought in annoyance.

"You must have spoken to Cameron."

"Who? No. Haven't seen her. Why?"

Mary Anne said, "It doesn't matter. It was just something we thought we'd try for fun." She hoped she wasn't insulting the woman.

Clare, however, did not look insulted. She looked as if she knew absolutely everything that was going on inside Mary Anne and was slightly amused that Mary Anne should be pretending things were…

Well, so what? thought Mary Anne defensively. It *was* something she'd agreed to do just for fun. Sunday, she'd thought that Jonathan had finally noticed her, but when she'd arrived at the station to talk with him about her being on *Life—with Dr. Graham Corbett* she'd found Angie and one of her bridesmaids there as well, talking about bands and reception venues.

"I really wanted to speak to you about your experiences as a midwife."

"Well, come in then."

The cabin smelled like baking pie, and Clare's dreadlocked daughter and two small dark-haired children, one still with baby hair and the other with a Mohawk, sat at the table snacking on various things and critically scrutinizing the face drawn on a gutted pumpkin. Paul Cureux held the carving knife.

Both Paul and Bridget Cureux had their mother's dark eyes. Bridget's seemed all the darker for the contrast of gold-streaked, albeit matted hair. Paul's hair was dark— as dark as Clare's must have been when she was young.

"One tooth!" said the Mohawk. "Just one!"

Baby hair sank a small hand into a pile of pumpkin slime.

"Let's sort out the seeds, Merrill," Bridget told the younger, who instead dropped pumpkin guts on the floor.

Clare looked pointedly at her daughter, who rose in a leisurely way to clean up and move the baby's high chair.

Squalling ensued, and minutes later Bridget was nursing the child and telling her brother, "It's cross-eyed."

"So are some of your neighbors," he answered. "In fact, it looks a little like…"

"That is not nice," Bridget replied.

Paul touched the knife to the jack-o'-lantern's face. "One tooth, it is," he said.

Mary Anne could not for the life of her see why Cameron should find Graham Corbett interesting when Paul Cureux was her best friend. He worked at the zoo at Chief Logan State Park. Kids loved him. He was smart. He was a talented musician and a performer audiences loved. And he was extremely handsome.

To forestall Clare saying something like, "This is Mary Anne Drew. She purchased one of my love potions," Mary Anne greeted Paul, reintroduced herself to Bridget, whom she'd met once years before, admired the children and used them to lead the conversation into the subject of childbirth.

To Mary Anne's relief, Clare did not mention the love potion, though her heart faltered when the phone rang and it turned out to be someone calling long-distance—from Woodstock, New York—seeking to buy one.

As Clare spoke to the person on the phone, Paul said, "Jake wants to make a documentary about Mom and her potions."

Jake was apparently a friend.

He added, "Sometime, I'm going to write a song about them." Among his other talents, Paul was able to create songs in front of an audience, sometimes at their request. He'd say, "Anyone have a topic for a song?" and hands would shoot into the air. Someone would say, "Buying a house," and Paul would come out with a hilarious song that covered everything from disclosures to competing offers to a spouse changing her mind.

At the moment, Mary Anne just wanted to get the Cureuxs, the second generation, off this subject of love potions.

But Bridget said, "You'd probably be happier if you drank one and got married and had children."

"You're scary sometimes, you are," he said.

"Mom has shown me how to do it," Bridget told him.

To Mary Anne's surprise, he looked less scornful than horrified. "I think I'll start drinking from a private water bottle."

Mary Anne swiftly steered the subject back to birth. "Bridget, have you helped your mother at any births?"

And by the time Clare got off the phone, Bridget and Paul had lost interest in the subject of love potions.

ON TUESDAY AFTERNOON, Graham put a stack of library books on the passenger seat of his four-wheel-drive Lexus and loaded the back with two weeks' recycling. There was not a lot of it. Bottles, newspapers, magazines, always neatly collected in the basement.

Graham did not like to go into his basement. This was why he put the recycling there. This was why he left the washer and dryer there. It was his basement, and he was going to make himself use it. So what if three out of four West Virginia snake stories involved vicious black snakes cornered in basements?

In any case, this was October. In October, it was safe to go into the basement without looking under the stairs and over by the hot-water heater.

They like hot-water heaters, a neighbor had told him. Not David Cureux, but the neighbor who'd told him about the baby copperheads in the jar. This neighbor had confronted a black snake in his basement and dispatched it with a shovel. It had taken Graham some time to pick up the fact that this event had occurred twenty-five years earlier.

Everyone also agreed that there were "snake years." Two years ago, when he'd seen the black snake and the copperhead on the same day, it had been a "snake year."

As he carried the recycling out to the car, leaves skittered past on the sidewalk and blew from the trees. It was time to put away the hoses. Five years ago, when he'd moved into the white house, he'd purchased some high-quality black garden hoses at Home Depot. For the past two years, he'd wished the hoses were green.

He started the car, and the radio came on.

"In the next ten minutes, we'll have local news on the city council's misuse of public funds and Mary Anne Drew talking about the magic of birth."

Graham gave the radio a look. He didn't want to hear about the city council mischief. It did not involve the entire city council, just one councilwoman who had taken a private jet to San Francisco and stayed at the Fairmont for a national conference on municipal planning. David Cureux was not involved, and Graham found it appalling that a man who would remove a venomous snake from a watering can before killing it in order to preserve the three-dollar can should be accused of squandering anyone's money. However, he wanted to hear what Mary Anne had to say on the magic of birth.

The local news carried him over the Middleburg bridge and onto the highway. He'd thought of raking before he headed out, but he had to admit he liked looking at the newly fallen leaves on the lawn. He could rake tomorrow.

"This week marks the hundredth anniversary of Logan County's first hospital birth," she began. "And I felt an irresistible urge to look at some of the births that have occurred here since then, including the births of both of my parents, my cousins, aunts and uncles, niece, my own grandmother…"

Mary Anne wasn't brilliant. This wasn't even one of her more brilliant essays. Yet somehow, she always seemed to vividly depict Appalachian life, mesmerizing her audience. Now, she revealed that her mother had been born in the hospital here during a snowstorm and her father at the hospital on a summer's day. She said that a cousin had almost died during childbirth. Not Cameron surely—must be another cousin. She'd talked to women out in hollows who had given birth at home, including one woman who talked about the convenience of breast-feeding her six children, saying, "I was the best dairy cow those kids could have had!"

Maybe the essay was uninspired, but Mary Anne was fascinating. Suddenly Graham noticed he'd driven past the recycling center. With a sigh, he continued into town. Library first. And enough Mary Anne.

JONATHAN HALE SMILED. "Good essay, Mary Anne. Just the kind of thing our listeners like to hear from you."

Our listeners. Was he saying the essay had no broader appeal? Possibly. They were alone together in the studio for the first time since his slightly altered behavior toward her on the weekend.

"Damning me with faint praise?" she asked.

"I think Graham's show will be good for you," he said. "You're capable of so much more than what you've done, so far, in radio. You have a great voice, great presence. And face it, you come from show business stock."

Mary Anne detested being reminded of this. Her father was past it, now. His personal weaknesses were no longer tabloid worthy, as they had been when she was a child.

Mary Anne pulled on her sweater-coat and swung her purse over her shoulder, then pulled out her cell phone to check for messages, lingering casually with one hip on Jonathan's desk.

Nearby, Jonathan leaned against the door of the recording booth. *All Things Considered* was under way. He asked, "Have you ever been married?"

"Absolutely not," Mary Anne said, not sure they'd been the right words or said the right way. "Why?"

He gave a casual shrug. "I guess it's usual for women to be more certain than men."

"I have no idea if left-at-the-altar statistics support that," Mary Anne said. "You know, one of my girlfriends was getting married at St. Patrick's Cathedral in New York City and she changed her mind."

"Really," murmured Jonathan, with mellow interest. "Beforehand?"

"No. Well, I mean, before she married him. Before she

actually got there. *He'd* gotten there, though. I sort of wondered if that was a last dig at him, you know. The total humiliation." She frowned, trying to imagine herself acting that way. "But probably not. She probably just realized she was doing the wrong thing." She squinted at Jonathan and was *very* careful not to sound hopeful. "Are you having doubts?"

He made a face. "Something like that. I just find there are more women I want to know better."

"You may not be a candidate for marriage," Mary Anne said without thinking. *"Ever,"* she couldn't help adding. Then immediately she backpedaled. "Of course, you'll always get to know other women—just not in the same way. I just mean—" Good grief, she was stammering. But she couldn't help thinking of her own father, her own mother, the pain her mother had endured—and probably *still* endured because of the antics of Jon Clive Drew. "Not everyone's cut out for marriage," she finally said.

"It would kill her," he said.

"No," Mary Anne told him. "It won't kill her. But it is insulting. I mean, to—" Stammering again. Her own heart knocking. *Come on, Mary Anne, even if he decided he did like you, he's already pretty much said he's not sure he's ready for commitment. And talk about being on the rebound.*

Not to mention that, at this moment, he was engaged to another woman.

"I'm not sure she's—" He seemed to be hunting words.

"Yes?"

"I think she may be…a little…narrow, for me."

Mary Anne would have seconded that sentiment heartily just a week before. But now, for reasons she couldn't explain, she was leery of doing so. Perhaps it was simply that, failing to win Jonathan through skull-duggery, she now wished to use only the most honorable means to gain his love. Which was pretty wild thinking, considering that until the past few days he'd never seemed to acknowledge her as a sexual being.

"Is it going to be a problem for you," Jonathan asked suddenly, "working with Corbett? I mean, you're going to do it, aren't you?"

"Why would it be a problem?" Mary Anne studied Jonathan's expression while she waited for his answer.

"Well, he clearly thinks you're something special, but I've always had the feeling that he doesn't really ring your chimes."

"Pushes my buttons, more like," she muttered.

He grinned. "Noticed that, too." He bit his lip. "It's partly her friends. I don't *get* them. You know?"

"You don't...understand them?"

"I guess so. I mean, they're all treating this like a royal wedding, and they're talking about what kind of house we'll live in and where our children will be christened, and it's not relevant to me. I wouldn't have thought Angie was that way."

"I don't think she is," Mary Anne admitted truthfully. "I think she's got something to her."

"Maybe *you* could befriend her," he suggested. "If you're seeing someone, we could double up sometime. Go to dinner. Have some beers at my place."

Mary Anne wanted to get down on her hands and knees and pound the floor. *No! No! No!* All this was because he wanted her to make friends with Angie? God. How pathetic her hopes seemed now. She said, "I wouldn't mind spending time with the two of you," hoping that her tone clearly conveyed it would never happen. "I've got to get to the recycling center before it closes. See you later."

Jonathan seemed to read her feelings. He nodded mutely.

Outside the office, Mary Anne leaned against the brickwork and groaned aloud.

Myrtle Hollow

"WE NEED THE phone books back."

We.

David Cureux's eyes quickly surveyed the area. Leaves falling on the cabin roof and over the grass, which couldn't be confused with a "lawn." No one was there. No Bridget's car.

Just Paul and his friend Cameron unloading firewood from David's truck, efficiently stacking it on the porch. Cameron was with them because, after they left the firewood, they were going to the Salvation Army to pick up some furniture and children's toys she'd found there for the safe house. Her presence was necessary, if they were to deliver everything.

No, "we" was just Clare, who had emerged from the cabin with an ominous sense of purpose, demanding that David bring back her phone books.

"They're gone," he told her, glad to join Paul and Cameron on the firewood job; glad he had a ready answer. "Took them to be recycled."

"The recycling doesn't leave the transfer station until Wednesday morning. This is Tuesday, and they're open till six. I called, and they still have them. We need them back."

"No," David replied. He wouldn't ask *why*. If he

opened the door a crack, she'd swing it wide and he'd be driving all over Logan County with a truck bed full of phone books. Again.

"Who is 'we'?" Paul asked. Paul hadn't had to move any boxes of phone books.

"For the schools. For the Crane-a-thon."

David did not ask. He said, "Then the schools can go get them."

"Muriel Aubrey, the peace artist, started it. Two cities in each of the fifty states are going to fold ten thousand paper cranes. Muriel is going to use them to construct a large paper crane to be a gift to the cities of Hiroshima and Nagasaki as a pledge against nuclear violence. The schoolkids who fold the cranes will also collect pledges from people for the number of cranes they fold and that way they'll raise money for cancer research."

"Sounds worthwhile," Paul remarked.

"So we need the phone books," Clare repeated. "For the paper."

David paused with his hand on a piece of firewood. His son paused, too, and their eyes met. David knew they were thinking the same thing.

David said, "Okay. Have to drop off my own recycling anyhow. Seeing that it didn't fit in the truck on my last trip."

Clare seemed startled. Taken aback. She'd been prepared for an argument. Instead, she said, "Thank you." Brusquely addressing Cameron, she said, "I spoke with your friend. She didn't mention the potion."

"What friend?" Paul asked Cameron.

Cameron said, "Never mind." Graham had drunk the love potion, which probably wouldn't do anything, but Graham already liked Mary Anne and Cameron didn't know why she herself felt so attracted to a man she barely knew. *Probably because I don't know him and can therefore believe he has a blemish-free personality.* Like one of the heroes in Nanna's books. But Cameron couldn't help asking Clare, "Where did you see her?"

"Here."

Beside Cameron, Paul lifted his eyebrows slightly. "Mary Anne?" he said in disbelief.

"Just forget it," snapped Cameron. "We weren't *serious.*"

"So who was it for?" Paul grinned, showing his pronounced canine teeth, which always reminded Cameron of Wolfie.

"I said, *forget it.*"

BECAUSE HE WAS ALREADY downtown, Graham stopped at the WLGN studio to pick up a recording of his most recent show for his personal library. When Graham walked through the door, Jonathan Hale was at his desk, frowning at his computer monitor. He nodded at Graham. "Ready to go on with Mary Anne, Saturday?"

"Absolutely."

"Good, I'll have everyone start telling our listeners. What shall we say? Dr. Graham Corbett and Mary Anne Drew on Dating Dilemmas?"

"Sounds fine."

"You want a specific focus for each week?"

"Yes, definitely. I'll have to finalize them with Mary Anne, but let's start with…" He thought suddenly of Mary Anne's annoying infatuation with Hale himself. "Unrequited Love."

"Or, Can't Get a Date?" Jonathan said.

"Different problem. Come on," Graham said. "Surely, you've suffered from unrequited love."

Jonathan seemed to think back, considering. "Not that I couldn't get over. No, when I was rejected, I've just kind of crawled back under my rock. Actually, that's not true. I usually got kind of pissed off. Decided I wasn't in love."

"You're speaking in the past tense," Graham observed.

"I'm engaged," Jonathan said.

Graham scratched his head. Now he'd heard everything. "You mean—" He tried it out slowly. "Now that you're engaged, you're never going to fall in love with anyone else?"

"I'm in love with Angie," Jonathan answered simply. "I'm a monogamous creature. End of story."

And this man had dodged bullets in a war zone. Graham debated saying more. But he couldn't *not* say it. "Jonathan, when you get married, it's not that you'll never fall in love with anyone else."

The station manager cocked a bemused eyebrow. His expression was assessing, forming judgments about Graham.

Graham finished, "It's just that you won't act on it."

Pleased by Hale's slightly disconcerted look, Graham collected his recording—and on impulse, the Killer Rabbit of Caerbannog—and left.

CHAPTER FIVE

WHEN MARY ANNE parked her car at the transfer station, the first people she saw were David Cureux and his son, Paul, and Cameron, who nodded at her, suddenly looking uncomfortable. They stood beside a recycling container labeled Mixed Paper—Magazines, Books, Phone Books, Etc. Mary Anne had some mixed paper. But all she could think about was that two of three people in that group knew she'd purchased a love potion, and she did *not* want the third, not known for his discretion, to find out.

Someone is going to tell. Then, it would get back to Graham Corbett, which was mortifying, and to Jonathan, which was much, much worse. The single comfort was that only she and Cameron knew for whom the potion was intended—and who had drunk it. In retrospect, it was all so embarrassing that when she thought of it she wanted to shrivel up and never be seen again.

Mary Anne climbed out of her car, grabbing her bag of paper.

Paul was punching numbers into a handheld calculator. "For ten thousand paper cranes at one phone book page a piece…Mom will find that wasteful, by the way. Ought to be able to get two cranes out of a sheet—we need either twelve Charleston phone books or—" he punched in more numbers "—fifty Logan County directories."

"Now," said his father, "once we have them, you take them to your house. I'll tell her I think you took them to the school. And make sure she can't get hold of you till tomorrow at noon."

"Why?"

"If she knows we only recovered two boxes she'll want us to come back and get the rest, so we can supply origami paper to the other forty-nine states. Then make sure you take them to one of the schools before she can get us cutting rectangles into squares."

"Right."

Mary Anne decided the men were so involved in their scheme, whatever it was, that she might be able to exchange a few words with Cameron and deposit her paper in the container without having to talk to the other two at all.

She had climbed the metal stairs that gave access to the Dumpster when Paul said, "Who did you buy a love potion for, Mary Anne?"

Her heart nearly stopped and her face grew hot. She stared accusingly at Cameron, who was glaring at Paul. "What makes you think your mom was talking about Mary Anne?"

"Well, Mary Anne's face right now, for a start."

What a maddening man. Why had she ever thought for one minute that Cameron should get together with him?

Mary Anne considered saying that they'd bought it to give to a friend at Marshall University who was majoring in chemistry—so that the friend could have it analyzed. But she felt as if her tongue had glued itself to the roof of her mouth.

David Cureux said, "Don't bother yourself about it. They don't work."

Paul gave a small choking cough, which seemed to indicate dissent.

Mary Anne did not want to do anything to verify Paul's accusation. She said to Cameron, "What are you doing here?"

Cameron told her about the Salvation Army and the safe house. Its location was a secret, which Cameron obviously believed both men would honor, understanding its importance to the peace and well-being of the women and children who took refuge at the shelter.

As Mary Anne descended the stairs, she realized that Paul's reaction had made her more uneasy about the love potion and about something she'd spent little time considering—its efficacy. She bundled her blazer close around her against a sudden brisk wind.

A Lexus turned into the recycling area. A man in a hard hat was approaching on foot and David waved to him, perhaps needing further help with his bizarre phone book situation. Mary Anne said, "Well…bye."

Mary Anne peered at the Lexus driver and wanted to dive into the nearest Dumpster and hide. It was Graham Corbett.

THERE SHE WAS. A good-looking woman, Graham thought, but that's what he'd always thought. Very attractive—yet her silly devotion to Hale, who could be a bit of a jerk, really annoyed him.

Graham eyed the white rabbit sitting on his passenger seat. Who *had* left the Killer Rabbit of Caerbannog for him? It had never occurred to him that Mary Anne might have done so. She hadn't struck him as a Monty Python fan. If she was a Monty Python fan and had left the rabbit, it didn't exactly seem like a sign of affection. More a wish for his untimely death.

As he turned off the ignition, he watched her carry a huge stack of collapsed cardboard boxes to a Dumpster. Great bones.

She was hurrying back to her car in a way that gave him the distinct feeling she'd spotted him.

He opened his door. "Mary Anne."

She spun, and he noticed, even across the blacktop, that her eyes were extremely green.

"Graham," she said with almost explosive brightness. "What a surprise."

A car maneuvered around his Lexus. Then a truck. The rush of people coming to drop off recyclables before the dump closed. As people parked and removed trash from their cars, Graham shouted a friendly greeting to David Cureux and his son, who were with Mary Anne's cousin.

Graham made no effort to lower his voice. "We're on for Saturday. The program will be, 'Dr. Graham Corbett and Mary Anne Drew on Dating Dilemmas,' and our first topic is Unrequited Love." He couldn't resist adding, "Do you have any insights on that?"

Around him, heads spun toward the person he'd addressed. A woman who was giving what-for to the guy in the hard hat nearly dropped an entire grocery bag of tin cans.

Mary Anne had flushed in a way he'd never have thought possible in someone with her particular California-girl coloring.

The only people who didn't seem interested in his question were David Cureux, now climbing into one of the recycling Dumpsters, and the man in the hard hat, trying to stop him from doing this.

Mary Anne recovered fast. A very small smile. "Men *always* love me back."

Graham could have sworn that the old man who'd gotten out of that '57 Chevy was turning up his hearing aid.

Graham couldn't help it. Grinning, he strode toward Mary Anne. "Actually, it's hard for me to see why anyone wouldn't." He plucked at her sleeve. "How about dinner tonight?"

Mary Anne glared down at his hand.

He removed it.

She lifted her eyes to his face.

Graham smiled...smiled with his eyes, too. His eyes were a sort of goldish brown that she supposed was called hazel. There *was* something appealing about this particular smile, Mary Anne decided, though she'd never shared Cameron's opinion on this subject in the past.

Graham Corbett had asked her out. Had Cameron heard? How could she not have done—she was only twenty feet away. Mary Anne stole a look toward the steps by the mixed paper bin and saw that Cameron had deserted David and Paul and climbed into David Cureux's truck.

Mary Anne said, "So sorry. None of the local restaurants have seats big enough for my butt."

"Then, you'll have to come to my house. I have a couch."

Graham noticed that behind Mary Anne, near the Dumpsters, Paul Cureux and the man in the hard hat were both shaking their heads and giving him a thumbs-down. *The couch.* Ah, well.

"For your information, I am a size eight and considered extremely slim for someone my height." She was, in fact, much closer to a ten on those few days before her period began, but she felt no remorse in giving Graham the size of her skinny jeans. There were usually a couple of days a month when they fit.

Graham said, "Mary Anne, I apologize for ever casting aspersions on that fine chassis of yours."

Two thumbs-down from Paul and the garbageman. David Cureux shoved two phone books at his son's shoulder blades.

Mary Anne drew her eyebrows together. "Does this ever work?"

"What?"

"This particular method of...courtship?"

"It's not *courtship*," Graham told her. "I just thought you'd like to have dinner."

His audience at the Dumpster—except for David Cureux, who seemed entirely disinterested—winced.

Mary Anne smiled. Great teeth. "It happens you're right. Lucille probably has it on the table by now. See you later, Graham." She spun away, whipping her hair with skill, and opened the driver door of her car.

This wouldn't do.

He followed her, though Paul Cureux and the garbageman waved their arms and shook their heads in a way that spelled, *No! No! Cut your losses, dude!*

She was in the car, but before she could close the door he caught it with one hand.

He asked softly, "Do *you* have the Holy Hand Grenade?" It was a Monty Python reference.

Her baffled expression answered the question he *hadn't* asked. She was clueless about the Killer Rabbit of Caerbannog.

She said, "Maybe you should talk to someone, Graham. Really," and shut her car door.

HE KNOWS! MARY ANNE thought in horror. Graham had somehow guessed that *she'd* given him Flossy. Or why that reference, which must have come from Monty Python? Her boyfriend had been as excited about the Holy Hand Grenade as about the little bunny with fangs.

Graham had asked her out.

Graham *didn't* think she had a big butt? Deciphering the car-related remark, she decided it had been a vulgar compliment. Though he had made that crack about the couch. Which could be read a few ways. She needed to call Cameron, to make sure Cameron was all right.

These things *did* happen in life.

And it wasn't as if the guys usually went for Mary Anne. Nine men out of ten flirted first with Cameron.

Would it be better to wait until Cameron called her? *We don't even have to discuss it, because I'm not going out with Graham Corbett.*

But it was looking plain to Mary Anne that Graham was not going to fall for her cousin.

As Mary Anne walked into her grandmother's living room ten minutes later and joined Nanna near her grandmother's chair, Lucille said, "You got a phone call, Miss Mary Anne."

Mary Anne blinked. Her friends used her cell phone. Where was it, anyhow? In her purse. She looked at it and saw that she'd missed two calls. She'd turned off the ringer and put it on vibrate, then left it in her purse.

Mary Anne asked, "Who from?"

"Man named Jonathan."

Mary Anne's heart gave a hard pound, but she quieted her hopes. He was probably calling to set up a double date so that she could become bosom buddies with his betrothed. Mary Anne did not ask any more about the call from Jonathan. This wasn't because she wasn't curious. It was because she was in her grandmother's house, and her grandmother would find such curiosity unseemly. In fact, Nanna looked entirely uncurious about the fact that a man had called her granddaughter.

Mary Anne absently answered her grandmother's questions about how her essay had gone. Why was Jonathan calling? *The double date,* she told herself again.

But what if that wasn't it? What if he was starting to be attracted to her, Mary Anne?

Don't get your hopes up, Mary Anne.

"What did you say?" She came out of a trance as she aimed this question in her grandmother's direction. It had been something about bridge.

"They had to cancel tomorrow," Nanna told her. "So I told them Saturday."

Saturday… "I can't, Nanna. I'm going to be on the radio. An hour-long program."

"Why, how nice!" said the woman, apparently sharing none of her granddaughter's fears that Jon Clive Drew's notoriety might find a new way to express itself in the next generation.

And Mary Anne didn't fear that—not exactly. It was just that Graham Corbett's being featured in the press as an eligible bachelor or heartthrob or anything of the kind made her skin crawl. She couldn't imagine why anyone would want to be famous. Rich, yes. Famous, no.

Jonathan…Jonathan wouldn't want to be rich or

famous. What if he broke his engagement with Angie? What if he discovered he liked Mary Anne after all?

Not going to happen.

As she went to her room to freshen up before dinner, she considered Jonathan again. Cameron had once told her that the reason a person fell head over heels in love— particularly the kind of love that felt more like obsession—was because of a need to incorporate some aspect of the loved one's being into oneself. This had always made sense to Mary Anne with regard to her feelings for Jonathan, because she *did* so admire his past as a foreign correspondent. She liked to imagine herself traveling in dangerous places, enduring hardships in order to interview those wounded by war. Not part of the conflict but damaged by it.

In the past few years, she'd managed to find something which seemed just as important in Appalachia. It was her work with the radio station that allowed her to do this, to interview the struggling single mother working at Wal-Mart, the people with water problems out in Mud Fork. Her essays let her write about those worlds, exploring the beautiful in the imperfect, the unique in the mundane.

Maybe she *had* incorporated that aspect of Jonathan into herself. So why wasn't she over him?

She listened to her phone messages.

"Hi, Mary Anne. This is Jonathan. I have a proposition for you. Give me a call."

A proposition? It sounded like something to do with the station.

"Mary Anne, it's Cameron. You remember we have the hike this weekend, right?"

Women of Strength. And Mary Anne *had* forgotten. She could only take part if she'd be back in time for Graham's show.

She returned Cameron's call first. Her cousin didn't answer, so Mary Anne left a message about the radio show.

Then, Jonathan.

"Hi, Mary Anne. Glad you called. You know, I think you may become our station's second biggest star."

After Graham Corbett, no doubt. She'd never heard Jonathan speak so ineptly before.

"That was a joke," he apologized. "And a lame one. Sorry."

Mary Anne tried to figure out what part of it was supposed to be funny.

"Hey, I'm putting together a plan for our election night coverage in November. I thought you and I would be on the air together."

"Me?"

"You have a strong intellectual presence."

Not that I've noticed.

He seemed to sense her doubt. "You're a good journalist. And actually, your essays are growing in popularity. I can see you becoming a female...I don't know...a cross between Noam Chomsky and David Sedaris."

She managed not to burst out laughing. But in any case, helping him cover election night would be good for her as a journalist, would further her ambitions. "Okay," she said.

"Good. Let's meet tomorrow. Are you free in the morning? Or better yet, how about dinner tomorrow night?" he said. "My treat."

He's engaged. Mary Anne didn't understand her own

qualms. She'd thought nothing of stealing him from Angie when she'd bought the love potion. But then, she'd never thought the love potion would work. "All right."

She hung up the phone with a mixture of excitement and guilt. Jonathan was suddenly being *very* attentive, and she liked the attention. But he'd asked Angie Workman to marry him. He planned to marry Angie.

So, he's treating me as a friend.

Was that true? Well, the dinner was about work, about the station.

She heard Lucille helping Nanna make her way to the lift to go downstairs for dinner. Nanna didn't come down every night, but obviously she was feeling well enough tonight.

Mary Anne's cell phone vibrated in her hand. Graham Corbett. Her heart thudded strangely, a reaction she didn't understand. "Hello?"

"Hi, Mary Anne. It's Graham. I want to apologize for asking you out in front of all the people at the dump."

"Were you asking me out?" she said, blinking, a strange dazed feeling coming over her.

"You didn't pick up on that?" He laughed.

He *did* have a nice voice. That soothing radio voice, a masculine voice with a unique resonance, like bass strings.

She thought over what had happened at the dump. "Not exactly. I assumed you weren't serious, given your past behavior toward me." She heard the hum of Nanna's lift. "I'm going to need to hang up, Graham. We're sitting down to dinner."

"May I call you later? Actually, I'd like to stop by. To run over some protocols for the show."

He wanted to come over—to come here?

"All right," she said, thinking about her clothing, wanting time to change. *After dinner.* "Seven-thirty."

"Great. I'll see you then. Shall I bring some wine?"

Wine? How would Lucille and Nanna react to that? Nanna would still be downstairs at seven-thirty, probably studying bridge hands with Mary Anne.

She felt a smile creep over her face. Graham Corbett, showing up with wine, perhaps anticipating some action on a *couch,* coming face-to-face with Nanna and Lucille. "If you like."

SHE'D SAID HE COULD come over. *You're doing all right, Graham,* he told himself. In his mind, he saw the long wheat-colored hair that she'd tossed so neatly at him that afternoon, and her black-fringed green eyes.

Mary Anne was beautiful. He'd spent years denying the fact by telling himself he didn't like the person beneath the pretty exterior. Why had he felt that way?

Well, there was her hero worship of Hale. And with that came the unspoken attitude that what Hale did as station manager and had done as a journalist overseas was inherently more valuable than what Graham did.

Graham couldn't agree.

But I do like her.

He was a little rusty about pursuing women. Since Briony had died, he'd dated, of course. But increasingly, he approached dating with caution. Even without asking women for dates, he received plenty of female attention, some of it hard to discourage. Perhaps because of his radio show and the resulting national attention, he'd been stalked by one local woman for nearly a year before her husband's work had dictated that she move to California.

And when he asked out women, he often found that they started calling him if they didn't hear from him again. Even when he dated a woman he found he really liked, something always made him back away.

Something? What had happened after Briony's death. Falling apart.

He belonged to the local gym and went there most mornings, early. There were women there, too, who'd hinted that they'd like to spend more time with him.

He shaved before going to Mary Anne's house. Dressed casually in jeans, flannel shirt and a fleece pullover. Then changed his mind, switching to a wool blazer. Grabbed the bottle of merlot that he'd bought on impulse. Because he wasn't a wine drinker.

No, not on impulse, Graham. You wanted to share that bottle of wine with Mary Anne Drew.

He knew where she lived and walked there at seven twenty-five, paused outside the brick house and gazed up at it. The porch light was on.

He climbed the steps and rang the doorbell.

Light steps inside.

The door was opened by a black woman in a blue dress, the sort of thing a nurse might wear. "Hello," she said. "You must be Mr. Corbett, here for Miss Mary Anne. Come on in."

As occasionally happened in West Virginia, Graham felt as if he was in a time warp. He stepped into a foyer so clean he could see the vacuum cleaner tracks on the light brown carpet. There was a hall mirror, and he saw himself, a tall and uneasy man come to call on a woman.

The woman who'd opened the door led him into the living room, where Mary Anne and a woman with white hair pulled back in an elegant chignon seemed to be playing cards at a small antique table. This older woman wore a sweater, slacks, heels and delicate gold jewelry.

Mary Anne stood up. "Hi, Graham. Come on in. Graham, this is my grandmother, Jacqueline Billingham. Nanna, this is Graham Corbett. And you've met Lucille?"

The black woman beamed at him, nodding.

He felt silly holding the bottle of wine, switched it to his left hand and reached out to take Jacqueline Billingham's hand, delicate, with its fragile skin. "It's a pleasure to meet you, Mrs. Billingham. And Lucille.

"I brought some wine," he said, feeling that perhaps bringing the wine had been the wrong thing. He'd known, in some part of his brain, that Mary Anne lived with her grandmother, but he hadn't envisioned things exactly like this.

"I can open that for you, Mr. Graham," Lucille offered.

"I'd be happy to—" But she'd already taken it from him.

Mrs. Billingham passed on the wine, but Graham and Mary Anne each had a glass. Graham asked Lucille if she would like some, and she said she might have a glass with them and she did.

Mrs. Billingham said, "Well, isn't this fun? How nice of you to come by. Now, you work at the radio station, don't you, Graham?"

He nodded. "I host a talk show. I'm also a psychologist in private practice in town."

"I know all about you," Lucille said from the doorway, where she stood with her half glass of wine. "My daughter-in-law, Ginny, listens to you all the time."

"Thank you," he said awkwardly. "I'm fortunate in my listeners."

The cards had been abandoned, though Graham had insisted that they should finish and had learned that it wasn't a game, that they were studying bridge.

Now, he sat beside Mary Anne on the couch. The couch was cream-colored with a floral print. This didn't seem a house where having a light-colored couch had ever been a problem. Nor was this a place where he felt comfortable teasing Mary Anne, so he asked Mrs. Billingham how long she'd lived in the house and learned that she'd been there since she was first married and that it was where Mary Anne's mother had grown up.

"Now, you're not from West Virginia," Mary Anne's grandmother said. "What brought you to Logan?"

"Actually, I'm from Tennessee. My wife was a graduate student at Marshall University, so I had a clinical practice there."

Beside him, Mary Anne jerked, and her wine flew onto the white couch and the light brown carpet.

CHAPTER SIX

HER OWN GASP she quickly disguised with exclamations of regret for the spilled wine. She leaped up to get something to mop it up with, but Lucille said, "You sit still, Miss Mary Anne. This is no trouble at all."

Of course, Lucille wouldn't let her do it. In cases of other spills, Mary Anne managed to do the cleanup only after some persuasion. *What if I get married someday and I can't get a stain out of a carpet?*

In her own mind, marriage had nothing to do with it, but this argument always seemed to appease Lucille, who would then give her tips.

Mary Anne had spilled her wine because she hadn't known that Graham Corbett had ever been married. She decided immediately that he was divorced and then caught herself. She'd jumped to the conclusion that he'd never been married, and she'd been wrong about that.

Anxious to cover the moment, she said casually, "Were you married long?"

"Four and a half years, which I realize gives me far less insight into the married condition than someone who has been married for ten years—or forty, as my parents were when my father died."

That was smooth, Mary Anne acknowledged. Though

Jacqueline Billingham would never show herself to be a woman who wondered if a person was divorced—being more the type to ignore the fact that *anyone* got divorced—Graham had decided to present his parents' credentials as people who had married for life and remained married.

"How long ago was that?" Mary Anne asked, knowing that her grandmother was probably thinking her too forward with these questions. Sometimes she wondered if Nanna was ever curious about anything, because so many things seemed beneath her curiosity.

Lucille, Mary Anne happened to know, was curious about many things, among them why Mary Anne herself was not yet married and when Jonathan Hale's wedding was going to be. Lucille would never suspect Mary Anne of any hanky-panky, as she would call it, with a man engaged to another woman. On the other hand, the possibility that an engaged man might make inappropriate advances toward Mary Anne was not beyond her imaginings. Mary Anne knew this because Lucille had asked rather coolly if Mary Anne had gotten that work question taken care of.

Mary Anne had found herself unable to admit that she'd be having dinner with Jonathan the following night. Instead, she'd simply nodded.

Now, though Lucille was absorbed in a quick and efficient cleanup of the couch, Mary Anne knew that she was just as interested in Graham Corbett's marriage as Mary Anne herself was.

Graham sipped his wine and said, "Briony died seven years ago."

Mary Anne didn't expect to be shocked by this—it was

one of the two possibilities for his marriage's end. But she felt it. It was sort of a heavy weight inside her.

Of course, nobody asked how she had died.

And even Nanna, Mary Anne felt sure, wanted to know. Graham didn't say.

Knowing it was incumbent upon her to say something to move them all beyond the topic, Mary Anne said, "I'm very sorry." She gave a just-long-enough pause, during which he only nodded, then said smoothly, "Nanna's been without Grandpa for fifteen years now."

"My husband was a physician," Nanna said pleasantly. "He had a practice on Stratton Street behind the Embassy Building."

"The brick office where the attorneys are now?" Graham asked, taking his cue as he was supposed to. "I like the ivy."

"It's hard on brick," Lucille remarked.

Mary Anne had a difficult time keeping her mind on the ensuing conversation, which covered both West Virginia horticulture and architecture.

Finally, Nanna said it was time for her to get to bed, for Graham to say that he'd stayed too long, for his hostesses to protest and for him to say, "I just wanted to speak with Mary Anne about work for a moment. It's been such a pleasure meeting you." He rose when Nanna did, remained standing until she'd made her way out of the room.

While Lucille helped Nanna upstairs, Graham and Mary Anne remained alone in the living room. Now she could indulge her own curiosity by asking how his wife had died, but maybe good manners had affected her more deeply than she'd previously realized.

Graham sat down again, not on the chair where he had

been but on the couch beside Mary Anne. Of course, he kept an appropriate space between them. If he was the kind of man who would put a physical move on her in an inappropriate way—and Mary Anne doubted he was that kind of man—then the atmosphere of Nanna's house would have forbidden it.

He said, "I wanted to bring you a packet of information about the show, but I forgot." He shook his head at his own mistake. "I'll bring it by tomorrow so that you'll have time to read it through before Saturday."

"I assume I'll follow your lead," she said.

"That helps, but there are some things you should know."

"Well, I've noticed that if someone has a real problem that they need counseling for, you tend to find a way to suggest that they get it."

"Not always easy," he admitted. "But as much as possible, we like to keep things pretty light on the show. The harder topics are for private face-to-face counseling."

"Right," Mary Anne agreed.

"Can I ask if you've ever had any?"

Mary Anne drew her eyebrows together. "Is it a prerequisite?"

He shook his head, again with the smile that she herself was beginning to find appealing. That troubled her. *Cameron likes him.* Though Cameron kept insisting that Graham liked Mary Anne, she'd not yet gone as far as telling Mary Anne to go for it.

"It's not a prerequisite," Graham said. "It was a personal question. Curiosity."

Cameron, Mary Anne thought. "Cameron thinks virtually everyone should have counseling."

Graham smiled but not in agreement.

She said, "The answer is yes. My father's an alcoholic and a celebrity, and I've found counseling helpful."

Graham nodded, wondering at all that was going on inside her. Wondering *everything* about her.

Now, she said, "I'm supposed to help Jonathan with some election coverage soon."

Graham blinked at this non sequitur.

"But obviously," Mary Anne said, "he won't be broadcasting that at the same time as your show. So it shouldn't be a problem."

Graham nodded, wondering why she'd brought this up. Was it simply to hear the sound of Hale's name? He rose. "Call me if you have any questions between now and Saturday."

Mary Anne said, "Thank you for coming over. It was pleasant."

She thought for a moment that he was going to laugh. Instead he said, "I agree, Mary Anne. I completely agree." He paused beside her grandmother's credenza, looked at a framed photograph there. "Is your mother in this?" he asked.

"Yes. There. And that's my aunt Caroline, her sister, and Aunt Louise, Cameron's mom." Mary Anne studied the three girls in dresses, posed with their mother and father. All wore full-skirted white dresses with satin sashes. Nanna's hair was in the same French twist she wore today; it had been blond then. "Caroline's the one who broke the mold." Mary Anne laughed. "She's the youngest." She moved on to another photo and showed Graham her own mother and father and her brother, Kevin.

Lucille came down the stairs then.

As Mary Anne closed the door behind Graham, Lucille said, "That's a nice young man."

Having forgotten for a moment that Cameron liked Graham and that she, therefore, should not, Mary Anne replied, "Yes. I'm beginning to think he might be."

Lucille didn't ask how Mary Anne could think any different. She said, "And he lost his wife."

Which Mary Anne took as evidence that Lucille, like herself, wanted to know how Briony had died.

THE NEXT MORNING, when Mary Anne opened the front door of her grandmother's house, she found a manila envelope on the doormat with her name scrawled across the front. She found a note from Graham inside, telling her that he looked forward to her joining him for his show Saturday afternoon. Thursdays and Saturdays were the days for his show. Also in the envelope was information about the show, including protocols for dealing with callers. It was part of a packet he probably had given to other guests in the past.

Mary Anne would make time to read it that morning. From noon on, her schedule was packed—with an Altar Society luncheon, a Daughters of the American Revolution tea, an artist's opening at the library and dinner with Jonathan. Jonathan had left her a message on her cell phone the previous evening suggesting they meet at the library and walk to the new Thai restaurant from there. Mary Anne was pleased with the choice. It was the kind of restaurant where you ordered at the counter, which made it seem less like a date.

Because she didn't want a date with someone else's fiancé.

No, she wanted Jonathan Hale to break his engagement to Angie Workman.

Is that what you really want, Mary Anne? Just twenty-four hours earlier the answer would have been...*of course.*

But suddenly, everything in her life seemed to be unfolding in ways she hadn't expected.

She'd just stepped back inside when the phone rang. She snatched it up to hear Graham ask if she'd received the envelope.

"Yes. Thanks."

"And I'm hoping you'll join me for dinner Saturday night at Rick's. We can talk about how the show went and have some fun, too."

"Oh," Mary Anne stammered. This wasn't a dinner invitation shouted across the tarmac at the dump. This was an invitation issued in a respectful fashion. Which meant she should pull herself together and prove someone had raised her right. *But what about Cameron?* For a moment, she didn't know what to say, as if she'd forgotten how to refuse dates. And she found herself blurting, "Thank you. I'd enjoy that."

"Great. Shall I make a reservation for seven?"

"Yes. Sure. Thank you," she repeated. *Oh, God, what am I going to tell Cameron? Why did I say yes?*

Mary Anne hadn't spoken with Cameron since bumping into her at the recycling center. Had Cameron seen what had happened there, noted the obviously nonplatonic attention Graham had been paying to Mary Anne?

Mary Anne punched *4*, which was her code for Cameron's number. Her cousin would be at work but might pick up anyhow.

"Hello?"

"Hi, Cameron. It's Mary Anne." *How am I going to tell her?*

"Hey. Has Graham gotten you to go out with him yet?"

The straightforward question was entirely Cameron, and Mary Anne felt almost relieved. Almost. "Um. I'm supposed to have dinner with him after the show, Saturday. I don't know why I said yes." *Forgive me! Forgive me!*

"How about, 'Because he's handsome and nice and intelligent and has the hots for me'?"

"Cameron, I'm *sorry*. Jonathan asked me out to dinner tonight, and I'm all off-kilter and not thinking."

"Cousin," Cameron said sternly, "your refusing to go out with Graham Corbett is *not* going to make him go out with me."

"And by the way," Mary Anne said, although it wasn't "by the way" at all, "how did Paul Cureux find out about the love potion?"

Cameron explained about taking firewood to Clare and what Clare had said to her and what Paul had then surmised.

"I guess there's not much client confidentiality in the love-potion business," Mary Anne said, feeling stung.

"Well, Paul says that they've been trained from a young age to be discreet about anything to do with their mom's clients, midwifery or otherwise."

"Obviously, that really took hold."

"Well, he only mentioned it to you," Cameron said, using an argument she would have found completely inadequate in any other context.

Mary Anne changed the subject. "Did you know Graham was a widower?"

"I think I did," Cameron said faintly, as if trying to remember.

"Well, *I* didn't." Mary Anne was intrigued about

Graham's wife's death. Did this mean she was interested in Graham? She *couldn't* be interested in Graham. It was one thing to be on his show, go out with him once and report back to Cameron that he was as disappointing as she'd always known he would be. It was quite another to become attracted to him. "Do you know how she died?" she couldn't stop herself from asking.

"No clue. Why don't you look on the Internet? See if there is anything there?"

Good idea. When she'd moved in with Nanna and started working for the newspaper, Mary Anne had arranged wireless service, so that she could work from home. When she and Cameron had talked some more about Jonathan and his date with Mary Anne that night, they hung up. Right away, Mary Anne grabbed her laptop and used Google to find Briony Corbett.

Immediately, she came across a foundation set up to provide money for athletic scholarships to needy female West Virginia athletes—the Briony Corbett Memorial Fund. The Web site included photos of a diminutive blonde spiking a volleyball over a net, sitting under a tree with a group of children, coaching a girl's soccer team. Briony was pretty—a freckled, wholesome kind of pretty. It didn't say how she'd died, but Mary Anne saw that she'd been twenty-six at the time of her death. Mary Anne read an obituary as well, but, once again, there was no information about how she had died.

She prepared herself for her time on Graham's show, trying to imagine what her role would be on the air. She wasn't subject to nervousness on the radio. Maybe there was an element of performance that was genetic. But that was something she hated to consider. It wasn't that she didn't love her father or didn't think he was reasonably talented. It was that he *always,* always, always needed the limelight. And he seemed to lack all common courtesy when it came to getting out of the way and letting others be noticed.

By the time Mary Anne arrived at the library she was tired, and she was actually grateful for this—it defrayed some of her nerves about her upcoming non-date with Jonathan. She'd used most of her free time between the day's appointments writing her weekly society column for *The Logan Standard and the Miner,* as well as editing pieces filed by other reporters. Though she had a paid position at the newspaper, several of the paper's regular contributors worked for free. And so she found herself teaching writing and journalistic technique to many of them.

She'd had time for a quick shower and change of clothes before dinner. Then she'd set out for the art opening at the library dressed in jeans and a long, lacy overblouse with a gray leather coat she loved.

The artist's name was Susan Standish. She painted oils of Appalachian life. A resident of Huntington, West Virginia, she'd been invited to display at the library as part of Logan's Focus on Mountain Culture series.

The opening was set for six-thirty, and Mary Anne arrived on time. The head librarian spotted her at once and drew her over to meet a small woman with reddish-blond hair in a long braid. Susan Standish was dressed in a raw silk jumper with a turtleneck beneath. Mary Anne had her SLR digital camera around her neck and said she'd like to photograph the artist with her work. But first she wanted to see the paintings.

Susan herself showed her around the exhibit. Mary Anne was charmed by her work. Coal miners with sooty faces, a mother and child with the thin, long bones she knew from this world, two grandmothers quilting, a blond girl on a tire swing. That last painting was labeled Not For Sale, but Mary Anne still leaned close to read the title. *Briony in Autumn.*

Mary Anne trembled, took a second look at Susan Standish, wanted to ask. Couldn't, because how would she, Mary Anne, know about Briony Corbett? Yet the artist could be the sister of the woman whose photo Mary Anne had seen on the Internet.

"My sister," Susan said. "It's from a photograph I took when we were young." She added, "She passed away."

"How?" Mary Anne asked without missing a beat.

"Staph infection. Strange, when we hear so much about antibiotic-resistant staph infections these days. But she never got sick. She wasn't sick. She was playing soccer, intercollegiate, and she literally dropped dead on the soccer field."

"My God," Mary Anne said. "I'm so sorry."

Susan nodded but didn't seem inclined to linger on her sister's death.

But Mary Anne had to ask, had to have it confirmed. "I think someone I know—" How could she phrase it?

"Graham?" Susan met Mary Anne's eyes and, seeing confirmation, said, "Yes, she and Graham were married. Did he mention it?"

"Yes. Yes," Mary Anne said quickly, anxious to show this woman that Graham had spoken of Briony appropriately—though why she should feel this need she had no idea.

"He had a bad time," Susan said. "Really lost it." Firmly, she moved onto the next painting. "Have you been up to Marshall? You might know this store…"

Mary Anne made notes as she followed the artist from painting to painting, then collected a copy of the artist's statement to flesh out her article. Out of the corner of her eye, she saw the library's glass door open and she wondered if it might be Jonathan. It wasn't, and she flushed. The newcomers were Clare Cureux, her ex-husband and Bridget, with a man who might be Bridget's husband, plus the two children Mary Anne had seen at Clare's house.

Mary Anne swiftly turned her back on them. She was standing in front of a painting called *Serpent Handling,* looking but not seeing, when a male voice said, "Fancy meeting you here."

Jonathan. She glanced sideways at him, annoyed as she felt her face grow hot. It was just that his "Fancy meeting you here" seemed flirtatious, a reference to their plans to meet. And he looked flirtatious, too, eyebrows lifting slightly as he smiled at her. He wore a black chambray shirt and a pair of corduroys; his dark hair was wayward, and behind his glasses, his blue eyes were checking her out—not lasciviously but with good-natured appreciation. Or so it seemed.

Mary Anne looked all around him, then peered around the end of the nearest library stacks. Turning back to Jonathan, she said, "I wondered if Angie might be with you."

"Ah…no. You and I have radio business to discuss."

"But to the opening…"

"I don't think she even knows about it."

Mary Anne wondered if Angie knew about their plans for dinner. But she couldn't ask. Jonathan had just reiterated that this was a business meeting.

Despite herself, Mary Anne said, "Have you gotten over your case of cold feet?" She smiled to make clear it was all the same to her whether or not he married Angie Workman.

"No," he replied succinctly.

"You will," Mary Anne assured him, not at all sure she spoke truly. "Look at this." She tilted her chin toward one of Susan Standish's oils, *Quilting Bee*. "I love how she does faces."

Jonathan made a sound of acknowledgment—then went on about his relationship. "Before we were engaged I thought I was the luckiest man in the world, that I'd found a simple woman who would bring permanent peace to my life."

The statement said much to Mary Anne. She was fascinated that Jonathan should *want* peace. "And now?"

"We're not alike," he replied. "The fact makes me nervous. You, for instance, are more like me. You might even understand me better than Angie does."

Mary Anne felt a renewal of the guilty excitement she'd experienced when he'd asked her to have dinner with him. Here was what she'd hoped for with the silly love potion.

Well, wasn't it?

He's still engaged to Angie.

And if that ceased to be the case? If Jonathan broke his engagement?

Words came to her unbidden, in a voice she knew well, a voice thousands of radio listeners knew just as well: *Imagine how you would feel with someone who*

*loves you so much that he wouldn't dream of saying
anything that could hurt your feelings... He's going to say
things like, "I can just imagine you in that dress. You will
look so beautiful. But you're always beautiful to me. I love
you so much. I cannot wait till you're my wife."*

Graham Corbett, who had a long history of saying
things that hurt Mary Anne's feelings, but who had
abruptly stopped doing so.

And while she couldn't quite imagine Jonathan Hale
behaving in the way Graham had described to his caller,
Mary Anne found she *could* see Graham acting that way.

She studied the transported features on the face of the
preacher who was holding two rattlesnakes in the air,
proclaiming. Jonathan had done a feature on snake-
handling churches two years before. There had been
negative local response, irritation that he had presented
Appalachia as a place filled with religious maniacs. It
hadn't helped that the serpent handlers were too frequently associated with crime. Finally, she asked, "So
where *is* Angie tonight?"

"She's with her grandmother. Her grandmother
doesn't get around well, and she and Angie play bridge
every Friday night."

Like Nanna and me. "You don't play bridge?"

He shook his head. "Not my thing."

Mary Anne tried to imagine what he and Angie had in
common and realized she had no idea.

Jonathan examined the next painting, a porch scene,
with women knitting. Mary Anne decided that she had
what she needed for her article. So there was no harm in
going through the paintings again with Jonathan, until he
was ready to go to dinner.

THERE SHE WAS. With Hale. Actually looking as if she was *with* Hale.

Graham wouldn't have missed the opening. He'd been the one who'd encouraged Briony's sister to send slides to the library. But even before he greeted Susan, his eyes had swept the area for Mary Anne.

There she was.

He had never felt so irrationally jealous in his entire life.

Turning away, he spotted Briony's sister and strode forward to embrace her. Susan kissed his cheek. "You look great," she told him.

He wore a wool sports jacket over a button-down Oxford-cloth shirt and velvety brown corduroys. "Thank you. So do you."

Graham tried to ignore the searching look in her eyes. Unlike most of the people who lived in Logan, Susan knew exactly what a wreck he'd been after Briony's death. Now, that vulnerability was something he wanted to forget. Who in the world would want to remember such a time of supreme weakness?

"Nice people here," Susan remarked.

"Have you met Mary Anne?" He had to say her name.

"The reporter?" Susan nodded.

"She's going to be on the show with me for eight weeks, starting Saturday."

Susan read what he hadn't said. Her eyes twinkled, and her reaction relieved him. Briony's family wouldn't resent his falling in love. They knew that it wouldn't change the love he'd felt for Briony.

That was when he spotted David Cureux and a woman with long gray-streaked black hair. His ex-wife? Graham had always been curious to meet her, especially given the tartness with which the physician sometimes spoke of her. Graham sensed that although David felt many of Clare Cureux's views were nonsense, he still considered her a close friend—perhaps his closest friend.

David saw his attention and nodded to him. Graham excused himself from Susan and went over to join his neighbor.

Introductions were made, including a young woman with dreadlocks, her bearded husband and two small children. Bridget—David and Clare's daughter—said, "You're the one who does the radio show with talk therapy."

"Not exactly that," Graham replied. "It's more like an advice show. I try to make clear that it's not therapy, or a substitute for therapy."

"Have you ever thought of doing a segment on love— falling in love?" Bridget asked, much like someone with a hidden agenda.

Graham told her about his upcoming series with Mary Anne.

"Oh, my God!" exclaimed Bridget. "*She'll* be perfect. She can talk about the link between magical herbalism and finding one's soul mate."

Graham frowned, trying to see a connection between herbalism and dating. He couldn't imagine Mary Anne Drew, a very mainstream sort of woman, involved in such things.

David Cureux said, "There is no connection, and there's no such thing as a soul mate."

"You're a skeptic," Bridget accused. She told Graham, "My brother and I grew up dodging intellectual missiles in the great cosmic battle between mystery and all things rational. The scale of this ongoing disagreement between my parents is, contrary to my father's point of view, divine proof that soul mates exist."

This intrigued Graham, who suspected he would weigh in on the side of all things rational and a world without soul mates. "What is the connection?" Graham asked. "Between herbalism and dating?"

"Love potions," Bridget said, as if it was the simplest thing in the world. "People do have the power to influence love, to shift its direction."

Graham categorically disbelieved this. He was, however, fascinated by the development of extreme viewpoints in children of high-conflict marriages. The daughter of David Cureux, a skeptic, clearly believed in something preposterous. Her father looked at Bridget with what appeared to be a mixture of pity, concern and exasperation.

After Graham had told them all it was nice to meet them and moved away again, he heard David tell his daughter, "I think I'd prefer you to believe that the earth is flat."

Bridget said, "But that's ridiculous."

Graham stepped around one of the tallest stacks of books to see Jonathan Hale touching Mary Anne's arm and asking, "Shall we adjourn to dinner?"

Mary Anne glanced up, saw Graham and reddened. "Hello," she said. Then, to Hale, "Yes. I'm ready."

Hale looked at Graham with an expression that seemed misplaced on someone's fiancé. There was smugness there as he smiled at Graham, gave a slight wave of his fingers and said, "Ta-ta."

To Graham, it sounded a lot like "Ha-ha."

CHAPTER SEVEN

"SO, WE'LL ROVE AROUND Logan, visit the campaign headquarters and interview candidates as they await the results of the local election. Our focus is going to be local. We'll steer away from the national election, although we'll be interrupting our broadcast for NPR coverage of that."

"All right," Mary Anne agreed.

"I think you'll be a natural at this. You're so comfortable interviewing people."

The food was good and inexpensive, and Mary Anne allowed Jonathan to pick up the bill at the station's expense. She didn't know how long such a restaurant would survive in Logan. The economy wasn't exactly thriving, and it was hard for any new restaurant to make a go of it. They sat at the table making notes of election concerns that would interest the listeners. Glancing out the window, she saw Graham step from his Lexus and come around to open the door for someone else. Mary Anne looked at her watch. Seven-fifteen. Yes, the opening was over, and that was Susan Standish getting out of the passenger seat.

Jonathan followed her eyes. "That's fast work," he remarked.

"They knew each other. He was married to her sister."

Jonathan lifted his eyebrows and looked slightly cha-grined, regretting what he'd just said. "Ah."

Mary Anne could tell by his tone that he knew about Briony Corbett's death.

He said, "That's a weird thing. But you hear about people dying suddenly from staph these days. I think it's hard because so many of the people who die that way are young and apparently healthy."

"Yes," Mary Anne agreed, trying to imagine what Graham must have felt when his wife died so suddenly.

"I think our Graham must have lost it for a bit."

Mary Anne looked at him, curious. It was strange to her that being with Jonathan in this restaurant felt com-pletely natural and, yes, somewhat exciting—yet it wasn't at all as she'd anticipated. She was wondering if Susan Standish was married, and she told herself that Graham was undoubtedly just showing her courtesy as a member of his late wife's family.

Jonathan said, "I didn't know him then, but a friend of mine knew him at Marshall. There were some pretty wild events. And general dissolution. He went to seed, missed appointments with clients, just about destroyed his life."

"Poor man," Mary Anne murmured, meaning it, yet not at all sorry that she wasn't in love with a man who went to seed among "wild events" and "general dissolution."

"I always had the feeling you weren't impressed with Graham Corbett." Jonathan had lowered his voice, even though the nearest diners were three tables away.

"I'm not. I mean—" That had been a stupid thing to say. She was going to be on Graham's show Saturday. She said at last, "I think it's hard for anyone to lose someone they love."

The rest of the dinner passed comfortably, though Mary Anne found herself disconcerted when Jonathan occasionally touched her during the meal. They were small, affectionate gestures, a brief squeeze of her hand as he laughed in shared amusement at a scene they'd both witnessed at the station the previous week, a teasing brush of his knuckles against her cheek. And as they occurred she found herself thinking, *If my fiancé behaved this way to another woman, he'd find himself unengaged pretty fast.*

Which led her to wonder if she really was in love with Jonathan Hale. No, more precisely, if she really *wanted* him. And she felt nothing but relief when they parted near her car, and all he said was, "See you Saturday."

SATURDAY CAME QUICKLY. In the days between, Graham called Mary Anne to run through a proposed schedule for the program, getting her agreement that an appropriate topic for the first session was Getting a Date. The eight-week program would be advertised as *Life—with Dr. Graham Corbett, joined by guest Mary Anne Drew on The Things We Do for Love.*

In no time, it was happening. They were on the air. Live.

"And we have a caller," Graham said.

"Hi, Graham," said the male caller. Mary Anne listened as well, with headphones on. "And hello, Mary Anne. I'm Luke. Okay, so I like this girl. Woman, I guess."

"How old are you, Luke?" Graham asked.

"I'm twenty-three. Anyhow, I work in a coffeehouse and she comes in all the time, but we're not supposed to hit on customers."

"You need to arrange to be where she is *outside* work," Mary Anne couldn't help interjecting. "Or you resign from your present position, get a new job, then wait for her at the coffeehouse where you used to work and tell her the lengths you've gone to just for the privilege of asking her out."

Luke laughed uneasily. "So you think it would be okay to ask her outside work, even though I only know her *because* she's a customer?"

"You're a barista," she said. "You're not a military official asking out a defense contractor. It's not a case of insider trading." She suddenly noticed Jonathan Hale outside the sound booth, a mischievous expression on his face.

"On the other hand," Graham remarked, "why is the rule in place? The coffeehouse management doesn't want to lose a customer because an employee asked her out and now the whole thing has become awkward."

Mary Anne thought about that. She said, "All right, then. You've got to choose between your job and the woman you want to go out with."

Jonathan Hale suddenly looked in danger of having his knees go out from under him and the phones went wild.

"Maybe she'll be impressed that you changed jobs so you could ask her out," Mary Anne added, a bit doubtfully. Color came to her face. *She* didn't think the barista should change his job, and now she found herself glaring at Graham. "Or," she said, "you could do what most people would do and find a way to run in to her outside of work. Then you strike up a conversation with her and see if there's any interest on her side."

Too soon, the next caller was on the line—a woman. "Graham, I want to know why you selected a so-called dating expert who would advise someone to betray his employer in order to ask out a woman."

Graham frowned at Jonathan, who had accepted this caller. Jonathan made a helpless gesture, one that suggested the woman hadn't represented herself honestly before getting on the air. Graham said, "And who is calling?"

"Anna."

"Anna, I think we're assuming that Luke's job is important to him and we're trying to come up with a solution in the spirit of what his employer expects of him. I think that probably his employer doesn't want him making a nuisance of himself to any of the customers. Asking a woman for a date when both are away from the coffeehouse seems a reasonable compromise in this case. Thanks for your call, Anna."

The next caller was with them in no time. "I'm Jack. I've got a coffeehouse in Morgantown, and, hey, I don't want my baristas picking up customers. Period. A girl comes in for a cup of coffee. That's what she wants. She doesn't want to have to field offers."

"Thanks for your point of view, Jack. And our next question about getting a date…"

"Hi, Graham. Hi, Mary Anne. My name's Jennifer. I really like this guy Adam, at my gym, but I read this book called *He's Just Not That Into You*, which said I shouldn't ask him out because guys don't like it. I want to know what Graham thinks about this and if he has read the book."

"Actually, I have, Jennifer, and I like it. I like it because it encourages people to think about how they really want to be treated in relationships and about how they themselves treat people."

"So you don't think I should ask him out."

"I didn't say that. And some men categorically *do* like to be asked out, and some find themselves enjoying a date with a woman whom they would never have thought to ask out. Nonetheless, there is something biologically interesting to men about pursuing a woman and winning her affection, and asking her on a date is a nice early step. Mary Anne?"

"I've never exactly asked a man out to dinner, per se," she admitted, "but I have said, 'Hey, want to go hiking sometime?'" She flushed, remembering asking Jonathan this once. She didn't dare look at him. "Usually, a guy will say that sounds good. If he's interested, *he'll* bring it up again. Or we might make a plan right then."

Graham said, "How come you've never asked me to go hiking?" He was clearly teasing, playing to the listeners.

Mary Anne said, "*That* should be obvious."

He laughed. "I asked for that, didn't I? So, Jennifer, I think you've heard it. There's probably nothing to be lost in asking him to go for a hike or join you at a football game."

"And maybe everything to be gained?" Jennifer asked hopefully.

Mary Anne thought of hiking dates, of coffee dates, of so many dates that hadn't worked out. She felt for this other woman, but also had a sense of futility. Why had she agreed to do this? How could anyone give advice on these topics, how could anyone give advice on anything?

The next caller was Sheryl. "I have the same question as Anna. What makes Mary Anne an expert on dating? *I* don't think men want to be asked out. Well, they might want to be asked out, but it's just for ego gratification. Men don't fall in love with women who ask them out, call them up or pursue them. I think it's biological, like Graham said. Men prefer to be the active pursuers, with women as recipients of the attention."

"Do you think that might be an outdated philosophy?" Mary Anne asked.

"I don't think biology is outdated," snapped Sheryl. "Obviously, Graham doesn't, either. Graham, aren't you less likely to fall for a woman who does the asking?"

"Actually," he said, "I've been thinking about this and I have to admit, my late wife asked me out on our first date. She asked me to join her and a group of her friends for dinner."

"Mate selection is the prerogative of the female," said Mary Anne firmly. "Even if he does the asking, we do the choosing."

Graham looked a little startled at this and Mary Anne wondered if she'd just imagined reading that somewhere, about mate selection.

"Thanks for your call, Sheryl," he said.

By the time the show was over, Mary Anne had the dreadful suspicion that the armpits of her silk blouse were soaked with sweat. Her blazer no doubt hid the fact from Graham and others in the studio, and the show hadn't been a complete fiasco, but still....

She exclaimed, "They're *right*, Graham. I'm no expert."

"Neither am I," Graham told her. "You did fine. Our reservation is for seven. Shall I pick you up at six forty-five?"

"Thank you," she said, thinking with relief about going home and showering.

CAMERON MCALLISTER lay on her bed, Mariah beside her, her running shoes and dirty socks strewn across her rag rug. She turned off the radio in the middle of the news broadcast following Graham Corbett's show.

Mary Anne had begged off the Women of Strength

hike, the herb walk with Clare Cureux. It had been a legitimate bailing out, Cameron agreed, the chance to be a guest on *Life—with Dr. Graham Corbett*. Mary Anne had done all right on the show, and how Graham had flirted with her. Well, didn't he always?

Cameron had asked Clare, "Okay, so what if someone has already been dosed with one love potion and we hit him with a different one?" Cameron wasn't sure *what* she believed about the love potions, but she *wanted* them to work. She wanted Graham's interest in Mary Anne to have been caused by the love potion. And she wanted to cure him of that interest.

Clare had said, "Who are you thinking of?" in that nononsense way of hers. It had occurred to Cameron first that Clare was afraid of her dosing Paul and second that Clare *wanted* Cameron to like Paul.

Cameron told her.

Clare had said, "He's all wrong for you. He's right for her." Then, she'd proceeded to point out a medicinally valuable grass, thus closing the subject.

So Cameron now lay on her bed, depressed. Depressed because the turnout for the hike had been just three women—self-defense classes definitely drew a bigger following, as did caving excursions. Depressed because what lay ahead was an evening during which Mary Anne would be on a date with Graham Corbett.

She reached for the nearby stack of her grandmother's romance novels, remembering when she and Mary Anne had talked about which classic heroine each of them resembled. Mary Anne had told Cameron that she was like Emma. Cameron had said, "An immature busybody, who thinks her mind is better than everyone else's?"

Mary Anne had said, "That's not how I perceive Emma."

Cameron had told Mary Anne that she was like Rebecca. And had been secretly pleased that it had taken her cousin two whole days to realize that Cameron had said Rebecca herself and not the heroine of the book, the second Mrs. de Winter.

She flipped through the books and selected *Behind the Cloud*—"The warm and thrilling story of a beautiful girl alone with the men of an Alaskan air base." Cameron was pretty sure her recollection of the tale had to be wrong, because she thought that the heroine had married the hero to save the reputation of a worthless relative and been so traumatized by her actions that she forgot the ceremony had occurred. She opened it eagerly, trying not to wonder who Clare Cureux thought *was* right for her.

THAT EVENING, Graham parked his Lexus in front of Jacqueline Billingham's house and hurried up the walk to ring the doorbell. He'd dressed in a dark jacket and was wearing a tie. Rick's, named for the restaurant in *Casablanca*, was one of two restaurants in Logan with a dress code. He'd once seen the maître d' surreptitiously slip a tie to a patron—Jonathan Hale, as a matter of fact.

Lucille opened the door. "Well, hello, Mr. Graham." Graham had noticed that shortly after their initial introduction he had become "Mr. Graham" to Lucille, rather than "Mr. Corbett." This, he knew, was a sign of approval, and he amused himself thinking of what his own mother might have to say about the fact. His father had passed away two years earlier, but his mother was still thriving in Memphis. She was coming to spend Thanksgiving with him, but he'd been toying with the idea of driving over to see her before then.

Mary Anne came downstairs. She looked fabulous. A black dress, above-the-knee length, with something he thought was called a sweetheart neckline. The back dipped low, revealing sleek muscles.

Graham swallowed.

Mary Anne said, "Good night, Lucille. I've got my key."

"You have a good time, you two," Lucille replied.

Mary Anne pulled the door shut behind herself as they stepped onto the porch. She was slipping on a black cashmere coat, and Graham helped, drawing it up over her shoulders. "You look absolutely beautiful," he said. "Have I ever mentioned how beautiful I find you?"

"Never," she replied, looking amused.

He opened the passenger door of the Lexus and held it while she got in. *Gorgeous legs,* he thought, watching with approval as she found her shoulder belt and pulled it on.

Graham carefully closed the door and was just sliding behind the steering wheel when a van bearing the logo of the local florist pulled to the curb across the street. He and Mary Anne both peered at it with interest, and Graham deliberately took his time fitting the key into the ignition.

A moment later, the delivery man hurried past them and up the steps to Mary Anne's grandmother's house, carrying a vase containing two dozen red roses.

Graham said, "Would those be for your grandmother?"

Mary Anne shrugged. "No idea."

He said, "You are popular, aren't you?"

She made a noncommittal sound but didn't look pleased by the floral delivery. Instead, she seemed tense.

"They aren't from me," he said.

Mary Anne, glancing at him, realized he was burning with curiosity about who had sent the flowers. She was curious as well, and distressed by the idea that they might be from Jonathan Hale.

No. Silly. He was engaged to another woman. He would *not* be sending flowers to Mary Anne.

Graham said, "Everything all right?"

"Yes."

As he switched on the headlights and pulled away from the curb, Graham wondered if Mary Anne regretted agreeing to come out with him. If the roses were from another man, maybe she wished she'd left her evening open.

He slowed the car again. "Do you want to go back and see about the flowers?"

Mary Anne glanced at him. Abruptly, she was frightened. Frightened because she liked the clean line of his jaw. He'd shaved before their date, she could see. He was so...*nice*. She managed at last to answer his question. "Of course not."

Graham examined her answer and smiled, easing the car forward again.

He nodded toward the radio. "Music?"

"I'm fine," she said. "What sort do you like?"

"Lately, world music. Especially from Scandinavia. I stumbled on it. You know Josh?"

Yes. College student, summer intern at the station, journalism major. Mary Anne nodded.

"He introduced me to it. People singing in languages I don't know, about legendary feuds. What about you?"

"Oh. Music?" She considered. "Sort of...folk music?"

Graham eased on with the conversation—date talk.

"What do you like to do in your free time? I've seen you on your bicycle."

"Probably not very often." She thought guiltily of Cameron's Women of Strength hiking trip and how she had canceled in order to be on Graham's show. Now, she was on a date with the man her cousin liked. The fact that *not* going on a date with him would never result in his asking out Cameron was no consolation. Cameron wouldn't hold it against her, any of it, but Mary Anne hated the idea of doing anything that would hurt her cousin.

Graham distracted her by asking her to tell him about her family.

This took some concentration. "Well, you know what my father does." She hurried on. "My mother is a church secretary. Her degree is in French. My brother, Kevin, is two years older than me. He's a chemist with a pharmaceutical company."

"That's quite a contrast. Between your parents."

"Yes," she agreed, her stomach tightening. "He was a miner before he began acting. He was an extra in something, and one thing led to another. They were married here."

"And they're still married."

She nodded mutely. Graham Corbett didn't need to know the details. There were many things Graham didn't need to know, because as her own mother would say, "It's no one's business."

"I told you my father's an alcoholic," she finally said.

"Recovered?"

She made a seesawing motion with her hand, thinking that the whole scenario would be impossible to explain and that it wasn't her family's way to talk about it anyhow. She turned to see Graham's profile. "What are your parents like?"

"My father passed away a few years ago. My mother is a novelist."

"Really?"

"Evelyn Corbett. She writes steamy novels about the South. All her characters behave badly—and truly, I have to admit. I think she's good."

Mary Anne took a deep breath, imagining what it would be like to live in a family in which twenty-first-century reality was acknowledged. *Like being freed from a cage.*

Nonetheless, she'd chosen to come to Logan and live with her grandmother, whose reality was the opposite.

With almost eerie perception, Graham asked what she was thinking. With a laugh, Mary Anne told him, concluding, "We're very refined on the Billingham side."

Graham asked, "What do your grandmother and your mother think about your father's alcoholism?"

"My mother wishes he wouldn't drink. I've never heard my grandmother mention it."

Graham smiled slowly. "Do you collude, to protect your grandmother from unpleasantness?"

"It's just not something that is going to be fixed by talking about it."

"Maybe not, but talking about such things can be healthy."

Mary Anne simply stared at him. She made no sign of agreement.

Graham found a parking space half a block from Rick's. Part of him wished he hadn't waded into these murky waters. But he knew more about Mary Anne now.

"You grew up in Florida?" he asked.

"Yes. I still miss the ocean."

He reflected that she must love her grandmother very much to choose to live in Logan with her, locked in the past in a home where no whisper of evil was allowed to pass through the door.

Their table at Rick's was upstairs by the window, an intimate spot near one of the fireplaces. When Mary Anne entered the restaurant with Graham she noticed that both men and women looked toward them, noticed them. The reaction accorded her less pleasure than it might have another time.

Why had she even brought up her father's drinking? It wasn't relevant, and she hated the idea that every un-pleasantness of family life had to be discussed and dis-sected. There were times when it seemed wisest to say nothing about some things.

They perused their menus and then ordered, were served their wine and some bread and butter. They talked casually of the renovation of the local movie theater, of that day's radio show, of the restaurant and its chef. But she was preoccupied.

"What are you thinking?" he asked at last.

"That not everything in life has to be talked to death."

He was buttering a slice of bread but lifted his eyes. "Yes?"

"Well," she said, "think about good manners—or dis-cretion—or what-have-you. It's for other people. Basi-cally, good manners come down to making things comfortable for others."

Graham smiled. It was unexpected, a slow smile from his eyes, from under that wavy brown hair.

Mary Anne felt comfortably warm under the grace of that smile. Perhaps because she felt so much...so much attraction, she downplayed everything. "You probably think it's just dysfunctional."

"I think there's a lot of truth in what you said," he answered. "About the purpose of good manners. Or maybe the *definition* of good manners. Briony and I had a friend who seemed to have been raised with no manners. She invited herself to dinner and stayed till two in the morning. I used to go put on my pajamas and bathrobe and walk out in the living room setting the alarm clock, asking Briony if she needed to get up at five forty-five or five-thirty in the morning. Briony would say, 'Ellen, you must be exhausted. We mustn't keep you.' But Ellen never got these cues. And you're right. Because good manners would have dictated that she wouldn't make us uncomfortable by inviting herself to dinner or staying so long that we needed to hint at her to leave."

Mary Anne giggled at the image of Graham in pajamas and bathrobe setting an alarm clock, all for the benefit of the dinner guest who wouldn't leave.

Graham's answering smile reached his eyes.

I like him. I can't believe how much I like him.

It occurred to her that this was the kind of man she *should* marry. And having been married once, Graham probably wasn't afraid of marriage or commitment.

He said, "I hope you can meet my mother at Thanksgiving. She's coming for a visit. I think she'll like you."

Mary Anne tried to imagine what qualities she possessed that would seem likable to his mother, the novelist. "Why?"

"Maybe because I do."

Her heart thudded. She considered asking Clare Cureux if the effect of the love potion could be for *her* to fall in love with the person who had drunk it. Not that she was in love. But she felt differently than she ever had before.

"I think I was a disaster on the show today," she said.

"You did fine. The danger, with that kind of live radio broadcast, is giving bad advice. You didn't do that."

"I don't think I gave any *good* advice. I couldn't believe how many people would have such strong opinions about the barista's dilemma."

"It happens sometimes. Don't worry about it. And keep in mind that what we're talking about is dating and we're not answering too many life-or-death questions."

"Well, it can feel life-or-death if you're twenty."

"True."

Mary Anne found herself breathing deeply, as if Graham's presence made her freer, released something stifling that had been smothering her.

Determined to keep away from the subject of her own family, she asked Graham about his education and where he'd met Briony. He'd done his undergraduate work at Yale and had met Briony at an intercollegiate soccer tournament. She'd been playing for Notre Dame. Then came the dinner date with several of Briony's team members. A brief long-distance courtship, followed by decisions to live in the same place, living together, then marriage. She'd been working on her master's in education at the university in Marshall when she'd died.

"What about you?" Graham asked.

"Columbia, actually. I really could be doing something more with my degree."

"Why aren't you?"

The question was bald. She didn't want to examine the *why*. But honesty niggled at her. "Fear," she admitted.

Strangely, he didn't ask her to explain, and Mary Anne was relieved. His silence left the way open for her to say more. "Writing is exposure. It's like being naked. It's easier to work…at the level I do."

After dinner, when they stepped out into the crisp night, Graham asked, "Would you like to walk for a bit? I always like that after a big meal."

"That's a great idea." They walked down Stratton Street past Our Lady of Peace Catholic Church. "That's where my parents were married," Mary Anne said.

"It's pretty," Graham said. "I particularly like the stained glass."

"You've been inside?"

"Many times."

Mary Anne was startled when a figure stepped out from the building that housed *The Logan Standard and the Miner*. A photographer clicked their picture, paparazzi style. It was Joel Naggy, a junior photographer for the paper. Though only seventeen—and a not particularly mature seventeen—Joel often got good shots that other photographers would have missed. Mary Anne said, "Don't bother. I won't put it in the paper, Joel."

"Wasn't going to offer it to you," he said. "I have bigger plans for that shot. Want to pose for one? How about a kiss?"

Mary Anne did not even want to think what he might mean by "bigger plans." "Go away," she said. She remembered, suddenly and acutely, finding a tabloid discarded in the trash one day. She must have been about twelve. She'd seen her father's picture, realized that he was drunk and had one arm around one bimbo and the other around another.

Well, Joel, whatever his pretentions, was not the paparazzi. Clearly, however, he thought Graham was big news. Mary Anne supposed he was right.

They continued walking and Joel eventually fell behind. Mary Anne remained silent.

"Not a big deal," Graham told her. "I'm not Brad Pitt."

"But didn't one of the entertainment magazines just do a spread on you?" she asked. Someone had mentioned it, and when she remembered who, she was racked by guilt. Cameron.

"Nevertheless," he replied. "In any case, I'm proud to be seen with you."

"I don't want to be in a magazine," she said. "Not for walking down the street with someone. I don't want to be famous. Or infamous. Or any of it. Having my byline widely recognized—I'd like that. Nothing more."

Graham gave her a surprised glance.

"I'm serious," she said. "It's a disgusting way to live."

Like her father? Graham wondered. He wanted to point out that her father's antics probably would have been agonizing for her even if they'd never been featured in the national press.

They were in the shadow of the awning of the Blooming Rose, the boutique where Angie Workman was manager. Joel had disappeared, and Graham turned to her. Gazing down at Mary Anne, he asked, "Do you wish I was Hale?"

She flushed, embarrassed that he should ever have guessed she'd been infatuated with Jonathan Hale. Was it as obvious to Jonathan? "Of course not," she replied, deciding not to point out that Jonathan was engaged to

Angie Workman, a reality that didn't preclude such wishing on her part.

Studying her face, Graham didn't believe her. She was still smitten with their useless station manager. He said, "Alas?"

"What?" she demanded, cheeks still flushed.

"Nothing." He shook his head, turned from her, and resumed walking.

Mary Anne fell into step, deciding not to take up the tangent about Jonathan. The truth was, the station manager was interesting to her. Graham never could be, because of Cameron.

He led her back to the Lexus and unlocked and opened the passenger door for her. As he drove them back to Middleburg, he asked, "Would you like to come back to my house for a while or were you hoping for an early night?"

Thinking of Cameron, she said, "I think I should go home."

"I meant to bring the recording of today's show," he said. "I have one for you at my house."

"Am I supposed to listen to it?"

"Sometimes it helps put you on track for next time."

This hint that what she'd done on his show hadn't been as perfect as either of them might have wanted made her reconsider. "I'll come and get it."

"Now?"

"Sure. I can walk home."

"If so, I'll walk with you."

Mary Anne had often admired the big white house where he lived. She liked the graceful wraparound verandas. A black garden hose was coiled near the front door. Graham seemed to do a double take when he saw it. "Neighbor must have brought it up here," he said.

"It's getting cold," she commented. Time to bring in hoses.

After a moment's thought Graham picked up the coiled hose, seeming to examine it suspiciously. Inside, he hung it on a door near the kitchen. "Cellar," he explained.

Mary Anne followed him into the living room, watching him turn on a light.

It was a comfortable room, attractive but unobtrusive furniture. Light-colored couch, in a pleasant pastel plaid. The curtains were filmy white. An oak coffee table. A stereo in an entertainment center. The couches and coffee table sat before the white fireplace. A fire was built, and Graham said, "Shall I light it? Do you still want to hurry home or would you like coffee? I have an espresso maker, and I have decaf."

Mary Anne, worried about her performance that afternoon, decided that this wasn't a romantic time and that she needn't worry on Cameron's behalf. Not to mention that Cameron should probably get over Graham, seeing that he was the only single man in Logan County who didn't think she was hotter than spicy Indian.

Graham made decaf lattes, and after she'd sipped from her mug, Mary Anne stood up to examine the photos on his mantel. She recognized Briony. The older couple sitting on a porch swing must be his parents. His father had been tall, with a thick head of white hair. His mother wore a stylish light suit and heels, her white hair in a French twist, her eyes dancing mischievously.

Mary Anne returned to the couch and sat. Her purse was beside her, and she felt her cell phone vibrate. She removed the phone from her purse and looked at the number. Jonathan Hale's mobile.

That was interesting. Could it be something important about the station? News?

No.

She decided not to answer, put away the phone and studied the room again.

Following her eyes to a game table set with a chess board, Graham asked, "Want to play?"

"Sure. But I'm not very good at chess."

"That's all right," he said with a smile. "I am."

HE BEAT HER TWICE—while also teaching her several useful simple guidelines for success—and then he said, "How about a friendly wager?"

"Do I look like a fool?"

"I won't ask anything too arduous."

She thought of Cameron. This was all getting very messy and she could not say, *I'm sorry, my cousin has a mad crush on you, and so I'm afraid your feelings for me may wound her.*

Damn it, they were already wounding Cameron.

Mary Anne said, "Look, I don't want you to get the wrong idea. I'm really not—"

"Into anyone but Jonathan Hale?"

"*No.* It's… Let's try to be professional."

He lifted his eyebrows, weighing what she said, then stood up with a shrug. "Professional, it is." She saw that he'd gone to fetch a CD, the recording of her first appearance on his show.

A siren rent the night, just as Mary Anne's phone vibrated again.

Frowning, she checked the number. Jacqueline Billingham.

CHAPTER EIGHT

IT WAS A MILD HEART ATTACK. No significant damage to the heart, the physician told Mary Anne. For the present, however, Nanna would remain in the hospital under observation. But they might send her to Charleston to see a cardiac specialist there.

Mary Anne was able to see her grandmother briefly, though Nanna was asleep. Lucille was knitting in the waiting room and talking with Cameron's mother, Louise, but after Mary Anne arrived she decided to go home, since she wasn't needed there.

"Does Cameron know?" Mary Anne asked.

"Yes. She was here, but she's gone now," her aunt replied. "She was called to substitute on the phone line at the women's resource center. I wish she wouldn't do that. Those are all such unsavory people."

Mary Anne studied Cameron's mother, who was very like her own. Both dressed in slacks and cardigans and polo shirts from JCPenney. Both were unpretentious, well-mannered and good as gold. Neither of them liked to acknowledge that bad things happened in the world—to anyone—or that a family member, for instance, might do something immoral. That her daughter defended women who sometimes had children by several different men from men who were sometimes alcoholics or drug users was all deeply disturbing to Louise—though not least because of her concern for her daughter's safety.

"Does my mom know?" Mary Anne asked now.

"No. I suppose I should call her." Louise started to take out her cell phone.

"I will," Mary Anne assured her.

Mary Anne returned to her grandmother's house to call her mother and let her know about Nanna's condition. As she made the call, she looked at the roses on the telephone table and plucked the card from among them. *Thinking of you—with news for you. J.*

She found herself thinking the initial almost pretentious. Oh, well, he occasionally signed notes at the station that way. What was the "news"? Her heart skipped a little. Would he… Would any betrothed man send roses in such a way to a woman who wasn't his fiancé? Could he have broken his engagement to Angie?

Her mother said, "Oh, dear. I suppose I must call Caroline."

The third Billingham sister. "I can, if you like," said Mary Anne, preoccupied.

Her mother appeared not to have heard her. "Now, Mary Anne, I don't want you bringing up that business."

It took a moment for Mary Anne to comprehend what "business" her mother meant. The "business" was the Billingham trait of never acknowledging or discussing unpleasantness. The last time their families had assembled Mary Anne and Cameron had decided to have an "intervention," speaking to Mary Anne's father about his alcoholism and womanizing and how it affected the entire family. Her father's repentance had displayed all its usual maudlin religiosity. And any improvement had been quite temporary. Louise and Katherine Billingham had been offended even if their younger sister had been supportive.

Mary Anne's mother continued, "None of us wants to upset Nanna."

The intervention had excluded Mary Anne's grand-mother, so this was ridiculous. "I live with Nanna and I certainly don't plan to upset her for any reason. No more do I mean to bring up Dad's habits," Mary Anne said, tight-lipped.

When she hung up the phone, she was annoyed and not looking forward to seeing her family. Her parents and Aunt Caroline would soon descend upon the Middleburg house.

Uneasily, she thought of Graham Corbett, whom she'd promised to call in the morning with a report. Well, she'd done her best to discourage him. But sometime soon she was going to have to talk to Cameron. She must let her cousin know how Graham was behaving.

Something very uncomfortable occurred to her. That things would somehow be *easier* if Cameron gave her permission to date Graham.

I don't want to get involved with him. What am I thinking? Jonathan Hale just sent me roses.

And had "news."

Again, she thought of her family's imminent arrival.

She should feel proud of her parents, eager for people to meet them.

Yet she didn't feel that way. Her mother was a good person, genuinely good, but so obsessively scrupulous about everything that Mary Anne had grown up with a deep sense of her own inner wickedness, a feeling that had only begun to lessen with age, when she'd found herself behaving like the person her mother and Nanna wanted her to be.

Yes, she wasn't crazy about the idea of Jonathan Hale—or Graham Corbett, for that matter—meeting her family.

HER CELL PHONE AWOKE her the next morning at eight. "Hello?" she answered sleepily, fearing new bad news about Nanna.

"Mary Anne. It's Jonathan."

"Thank you for the flowers," she said. "They're lovely."

"As are you," he replied. "And I have something to tell you. I wanted you to be the first to know. Angie and I have broken off our engagement."

Mary Anne's heart struck one hard note, then raced. How could this be happening? After everything she'd tried, even the desperation of the love potion? And he wanted *her* to be the first to know?

She knew how she *should* feel—ecstatic. But that wasn't how she felt. The Billingham side of her knew that breaking up someone's engagement was just a hair on the right side of home-wrecking, and she felt her character had been branded. She could have guessed beforehand that if the event occurred she would have these misgivings. Hadn't Clare Cureux warned her? But she'd never believed it would happen, had never even believed that the love potion would work—and then the wrong person had drunk it.

But if his attachment to Angie was this shallow…

"I'm surprised," she finally managed to say. "Was this a mutual thing?"

His silence seemed a kind of hedging. "No. But I realized I'd gotten into it too quickly and should break things off before we went any further."

Mary Anne told herself that *she* wasn't the reason behind this breakup, and that if Jonathan was so unsure—well, it must be for the best. "Is Angie all right?" she asked.

"Sure. Sure." He sounded as if he was trying to convince himself.

She told him about Nanna and he asked if there was anything he could do, then asked if she was free that evening.

"Maybe," she said, trying not to think about the fact her parents would be in town. "What did you have in mind?"

"Cooking dinner for you."

That meant she would go to *his* house. "If I don't need to be with my grandmother, I'd like that," she said. As she hung up, she wondered why Clare Cureux had been so insistent about the right person drinking the love potion. Clearly, Jonathan was becoming attracted to her *without* benefit of the potion. She must simply forget about the love potion. She only wished she could persuade Cameron and everyone else who knew about it—a list that now seemed to include at least one of Clare Cureux's children—to do the same.

MARY ANNE'S FIRST excursion of the day was to the hospital to see Nanna. She met Cameron there. After each had visited briefly with their grandmother, they stopped in Grounds for Friendship, Stratton Street's coffeehouse. They ordered espressos and when they were seated at a table in the corner near the front window Mary Anne wasted no time in telling her cousin of Jonathan and Angie's broken engagement.

Cameron exclaimed, "You're kidding. Did he say why?"

"Not really, but we have a date tonight."

Cameron seemed pleased by this, yet she still asked, "How did your date with Graham go?"

Mary Anne could understand all the feeling behind the question. She wanted to reassure her cousin yet believed that there was no point in reassuring her. Graham was interested in Mary Anne, not Cameron. So rather than deceive Cameron, she shrugged. "It was fine." It was on the tip of her tongue to say, *He doesn't do anything for me.* Yet this wasn't precisely true. Instead, she said, "I don't want to be with anyone famous and while, as he says, he's not Brad Pitt, I still don't like it."

"It's not like he can help it, Mary Anne," Cameron pointed out.

"It's not like *I* can help how I feel about it, either." But was that true? Graham *wasn't* a movie star or a teen idol. More importantly, he wasn't an alcoholic like her father. He seemed a moderate person. Well, except, apparently, when his wife had died. Jonathan's description of Graham's behavior had sounded so like the kind of thing her father did without reason at least once a year.

"So you're still not attracted to him?" Cameron asked.

Mary Anne wanted to say that she wasn't—but that wouldn't have been true.

Cameron seemed to read her hesitation. "Look, if you're interested in him, go for it. It's not like your turning him down is going to make him go for me."

Having received this release to do as she pleased, Mary Anne said, "With Jonathan free, nothing's likely to happen between Graham and me."

Cameron nodded thoughtfully. "It doesn't speak to

the effectiveness of Clare's love potions, does it? Though it *does* seem to be working on Graham."

Mary Anne was exasperated abruptly. "How can you think it worked? They're ridiculous."

"I don't think they are," Cameron said, looking as if she wished she could agree with Mary Anne. "Paul swears that every time one has been used, the people have ended up together."

"Look, even if that were true," Mary Anne said, "history argues against it. Probably the most famous love-potion-gone-wrong story in the world is that of Tristan and Isolde and *they* didn't end up together, not in the way you mean. They both ended up dead, but I hardly think that's the same thing.

"In all of life, people end up married to the 'wrong' people." She held up two fingers of each hand to put quotes around wrong. "Life just isn't something that can be manipulated with love potions—human feelings certainly can't be."

"I wish I believed that," Cameron said wryly.

Understanding, Mary Anne said, "He used to flirt with me before the potion, Cameron. You can't blame the love potion for what he's doing."

"No. I'd like to blame it for what you're doing," Cameron said.

Mary Anne's espresso was halfway to her lips. She lowered the cup. "What is it I'm doing?"

"Encouraging him?"

"You just told me I could!"

"I know. What I mean is, I think you're falling for him, too," Cameron explained.

"That is *not* happening," Mary Anne assured her. "I

don't positively dislike him the way I used to, but he's still too much of a celebrity for me and it appears he has been known to act like my father on occasion." She didn't mention the circumstances of the occasion—the sudden death of his young wife.

"Well, time will tell," Cameron remarked, with less than her usual optimism.

Mary Anne wanted to say something to make things right between them, but only time could cure Cameron of her infatuation with Graham Corbett. She settled for, "What I'm looking forward to is seeing Jonathan tonight and finding out all about him and Angie."

WHEN SHE RETURNED to Nanna's house, the car in the driveway was not Nanna's—which Lucille always garaged, in any case—but a vintage aqua Thunderbird. Mary Anne knew the car and experienced a whole host of feelings as she parked at the curb in front of the house. She had always liked Aunt Caroline, and when she was young she'd wished Caroline had been her mother. But Aunt Caroline's arrival presaged the arrival of Mary Anne's own parents, something to which she wasn't looking forward.

As she slung her purse over her shoulder and stepped away from her car, the front door of the house opened and the familiar figure came out, all voluptuous angles and high heels and French twist and artfully applied makeup and exuberance. In her arms was a white Maltese as perfectly groomed as she was. "Hi, chicken!" called Aunt Caroline, in her unforgettable husky sandpaper voice, nearly running down the front steps.

Mary Anne hurried to hug Caroline, who was as tall

as she was, and to give a pat to the dog. "Hello, Paris. How are you, little sweetie?"

"Good as gold. Did I tell you she won her major? She's a champion now. Breeders were thrilled, of course."

"That's great," Mary Anne said. If her grandmother had been at home, she would have disapproved of the dog's presence, worried and complained but allowed it. Mary Anne could never see the problem. Paris was so clean and well-behaved she was hardly a dog at all.

Caroline was fifty, Mary Anne knew, and as always she looked good. Her suit was a 1940s style silk shantung thing in an earthy, unnamable greenish brown, and her body might have been poured into it. Only one thing showed her age. Though her makeup was impeccable, her hair almost platinum in its twist, her skin showed her to be the smoker she was. Even now, she clutched a cigarette and lighter.

"Mary Anne, you're prettier every time I see you."

"You, too, Aunt Caroline."

Her aunt made a sound like, "Pshaw!" Then she said, "I was just coming out for a smoke, but I think I need my coat."

Mary Anne gave her a gentle shake. "You need to stop."

"Chicken, it's just one of my real pleasures."

Throughout Mary Anne's childhood, Aunt Caroline had breezed into the family home once a year, bringing Mary Anne the beautiful dolls her mother had said were too expensive and refused to buy her. It was Caroline who had taken Mary Anne shopping in Orlando for the kind of clothes her mother thought were too sexy. It was Caroline who had made Mary Anne want to see more of the world. Caroline, lucratively widowed once and then divorced three times, the latter a fact Mary Anne had never heard Nanna mention. She'd felt her own mother's disapproval of the first divorce, heard the sighs over the second, seen her lips tighten at news of the third. Nanna never mentioned her youngest daughter's marital status.

All that bothered Mary Anne, though, were the hints sometimes dropped that Caroline, rather than Katherine Billingham, had been Jon Clive Drew's first choice decades earlier.

"Now, if I get my coat, will you sit out here with me?"

"Does that make me complicit in your smoking?" Mary Anne asked.

"I'll be having this cigarette with or without you."

"Then, of course I'll stay outside with you." Inside Mary Anne a shell was forming, the protective shell that hardened whenever her family assembled. Her family, Cameron excluded. Except that now even Cameron seemed like a problem.

"Here," Caroline said, setting down the dog. "Hold her lead. I'll have my ciggie and then take her for walkies."

A few minutes later, they sat on Nanna's porch swing, and Mary Anne asked, "Have you seen Nanna?"

"I have," Caroline said. "She looks awfully good for someone with a heart condition." Her aunt paused, then demanded, "Now, is there a nice man in your life yet?"

Mary Anne considered. "I'm not sure." She told Caroline all about Jonathan and then said, "Oh, and I had a date with Graham Corbett."

"The fellow with the radio show?"

"Yes. Have you heard it? I'm being his guest for a few weeks. I'm supposedly a dating expert."

"And you're dating him?"

"We've been on one date. Cameron likes him." She rushed on. "What about you?"

"I'm finding I like living alone, Mary Anne. Well, me and Paris. Truthfully, I haven't found a man who makes a better companion than a dog does. Is your mother coming?"

"I think they're both coming." And God knew what her father would get up to while he was in town.

As though reading her mind, Caroline said, "He's a handsome devil, Jon Clive is."

"Yes," Mary Anne agreed. "I wonder if he was ever different."

Caroline's tone turned a little bitter, for her sister's lot Mary Anne was sure. "No, he never was. Not since I've known him."

But Katherine Billingham had married him. And like her mother before her, she did not believe in divorce.

Mary Anne thought of all the times in her life when her father should have been responsible, could have been someone of whom she could be proud. Instead—humiliating exhibitions of drunkenness, womanizing and public repentance.

Maybe she could arrange to leave the city, or the country, while her parents were in Logan.

Caroline added, "Chicken, if your daddy's behavior is really eating at you, you might want to talk to a counselor. Helps everyone, you know."

"I've spent more time in therapy than I did in college," Mary Anne snapped. Then, forcing her tone back into a more civil state, she said, "Have you been in therapy ever?"

"Why, sure, honey. Quite a few times. Now, isn't your Graham Corbett in that line of work?"

"He can't be my therapist—we're on his show together. Anyhow, I know him personally. And he's not *my* Graham Corbett. As I said, I'm going to Jonathan's tonight."

"Yes, well, don't be in a hurry to jump on that raft.
He's on the rebound," Caroline warned. "And I hate it that
he broke up with his fiancée one minute and is chasing
you the next. Anyhow, I wasn't suggesting Graham
Corbett as your counselor," Caroline answered with a
laugh. "I just wanted to know more about him."

"His life is an open book, just like that of every other
well-known person."

Caroline rolled her eyes at this, then stubbed out her
cigarette. "Well, that went by too fast." The cigarette. "I'll
just put this inside in the trash, and we'll take Paris for
her walkies. And when we come back we'll have a drink
and scare up some dinner."

"I'm going to Jonathan's for dinner."

"That's right, I forgot."

Soon Caroline and Mary Anne started down the front
steps, and Paris took them at a dainty but enthusiastic
pace, stretching to the end of the slender lead.

Caroline started in the direction they usually went to
walk her dog when she was visiting. Around the block.
Which would entail going past Graham's house. Mary
Anne didn't mind Caroline knowing where Graham lived.
Caroline would never embarrass her. But Mary Anne did
feel an instinct to conceal the fact from her parents.

His car came up the street just as they were almost
past his house.

Mary Anne flushed with embarrassment. Would he
think she'd been keen to show off his house to her aunt?
Would he think she was just going past his house because
she had a crush on him, or something like that?

*Stupid, Mary Anne. Of course not. You've been on a
date with him.*

He parked and got out of the car and immediately waved and crossed the leaf-strewn lawn to them. He crouched briefly to let Paris sniff his hand, then petted her. Standing again, he said, "I'm Graham Corbett," and held out his hand to Caroline.

"Graham, this is my aunt, Caroline Jackson." Caroline had taken her first husband's name and never dropped it.

"I'm glad to meet some of Mary Anne's family."

"You'll be seeing more of us than you want," Caroline replied with a laugh. "When are your folks getting in, Mary Anne?"

Damn, why had she mentioned it to Graham?

"Tonight," Mary Anne replied.

"Charleston?" Graham asked.

"Oh, I'm sure their plane's long since on the ground. They planned to rent a car," Mary Anne answered in a rush.

"I hope I have a chance to meet them while they're here," Graham told her. "How is your grandmother?"

"Looking like she could do a few laps around the block," Caroline replied for Mary Anne.

"Why don't you join us for dinner tomorrow, Graham?" Caroline offered. "And you can tell us about your interesting work."

No! No! No! Mary Anne wanted to scream. Her parents would be there, exposing their awkward behavior to Graham.

"I'd like that. Shall I bring anything?"

"How about a nice bottle of wine? Let's plan on chicken—something to go with that."

"Wonderful," he answered.

Mary Anne rarely prayed, but she did then. *Let my family not humiliate me in front of this man.*

MARY ANNE'S MOTHER called to say that the Florida weather had kept their plane on the ground. "We were waiting for hours. Now we've decided to drive, but Caroline said Mother is in no immediate danger so we're not leaving till tomorrow morning. That way, we'll be fresh."

"Okay," Mary Anne agreed, hoping they wouldn't arrive in Middleburg till after dinner, till Graham was gone.

She apologized earnestly to her aunt for leaving her alone her first night, but Caroline said Cameron had promised to come over, knowing that Mary Anne would be out. "She and I are going to have a girl night!"

"Good," Mary Anne said, uncertain why the plan should make her uneasy.

She left for Jonathan's at six-thirty, in the time frame he'd suggested.

Jonathan Hale lived downtown in a brick house similar to Nanna's. He owned the house, having bought it when he first moved to Logan and took the job as station manager.

Mary Anne smelled coals on the grill as she got out of her car at the curb. It was a warm evening for autumn, and she found Jonathan on the side porch, checking the fire and drinking a beer.

He looked up. "Oh, hi." He appeared mildly disheveled, in a flannel shirt with the tails hanging out of his jeans and wearing socks without shoes. His hair looked almost slept-on, yet was still appealing.

"Hi," Mary Anne replied, aware of the contrast in her own appearance. She'd worn jeans, but also had on high platform shoes and a long sweater the color of her eyes, plus large dangling earrings.

Jonathan made no comment whatsoever, but instead just held the side door open for her. "Come on in. Want a beer?"

They sat on his porch drinking from bottles and eating salad while the salmon grilled.

"I feel like I'm freed from execution," Jonathan said abruptly.

It took a moment for Mary Anne to realize that he was referring to his broken engagement. "Then, it seems like you've done the right thing," she finally answered.

"She's all wrong for me," he said.

"How is she doing?" Mary Anne asked. She remembered discussions of flowers and bridesmaids' dresses and was sure that Angie wasn't sharing his glee.

He looked sober momentarily. "She's okay. I talked to her again today. I thought we'd take a break from each other. She says she has no interest in dating me again. So—I guess that's that."

Mary Anne detected no regret in his tone.

"Tell me more about you," he said. "I've known you since I came to Logan, yet I still feel as though I don't really know you."

"I grew up in Florida." She ran through her educational and work resumé.

"Could you live in the city again?" he asked, meaning New York.

"Sure."

"Angie could never imagine living anywhere but here."

Mary Anne didn't answer.

The salmon was perfect. When they finished eating, Jonathan suggested going inside to listen to some new music one of the disc jockeys had given him.

But no sooner was she seated on the plaid couch in his

comfortable living room, than he sat beside her, put his arms around her and kissed her soundly on the lips.

Mary Anne was dumbfounded. She didn't quite want to kiss him back, yet she felt she *should* kiss him back. She moved away, and he grinned at her.

She did allow him to kiss her again and did kiss him back, more accustomed now to the idea. His hands stroked her cheek and her hair, and it seemed romantic yet also…practiced. Expert, almost.

Mary Anne couldn't account for her own confusion. She'd liked him—thought herself in love with him—for years. And now he was responding to her. Was it that she thought he'd had more than just the two beers he'd drunk since she'd arrived? That could be part of it.

He said, "Want to go upstairs?"

"No," Mary Anne said abruptly. "Not now. As you said earlier, we barely know each other."

"But we *do* know each other," he said. "And, face it, we've been eyeing each other for years."

At least he hadn't said that *she'd* had her eye on *him* for years, which was closer to the truth.

"You've just broken up with Angie," Mary Anne reminded him. "This is all a little soon for me."

He seemed to consider her, then nodded slowly. "How about a movie?"

"My aunt is—" But Cameron was with Caroline. "All right."

He put *Midaq Alley* in the DVD player, and Mary Anne soon found that reading subtitles was hard going while dealing with Jonathan's nonstop caresses. *This is what I want,* she kept telling herself. Yet the situation seemed a little out of control, and only lessened somewhat whenever Salma Hayek came on the screen to distract him.

When she finally left, it was after several more long, tender kisses from Jonathan and his promise, "I'll call you tomorrow."

On the way home, she smiled, telling herself that she was finally receiving what she wanted.

BY SIX THE FOLLOWING NIGHT, the hour Mary Anne had insisted on for dinner, her parents had still not arrived. This was what she'd hoped for, why she'd argued against Caroline's suggested dinnertime of seven.

So, she, Aunt Caroline and Graham sat down together, and Mary Anne hoped her parents wouldn't arrive until Graham had left. In the meantime, everything was perfect.

"Now, I read all her books!" Caroline exclaimed delightedly when Graham revealed that his mother was the author Evelyn Corbett. "I just love her people—they're always getting into scrapes, doing all those things people do. My mother, now, she wouldn't look twice at a book like that."

"Sex," Mary Anne said.

"Violence," Caroline added.

"Reality," Mary Anne concluded. The evening was going fine. She and Caroline and Graham were sharing chicken and some wonderful zucchini and squash and an excellent merlot. It was fun to have Graham here with Caroline—Caroline who had been raised, as Mary Anne's mother had, to make other people feel comfortable.

Except that Mary Anne sometimes believed her mother had missed the fundamental point of courtesy. Because her propriety always let people know when *she* was experiencing discomfort, discomfort at the mention of some unpleasant reality. Something like the fact that Mary Anne's brother, Kevin, and his girlfriend, Kendra, lived together but were not married. Something normal.

"Did Hale get a hold of you?" Graham asked casually. "I stopped by the studio this morning, and he mentioned that he'd been trying to reach you."

"Yes," Mary Anne said. Jonathan had wanted to get together again tonight, but she'd said she had plans. He'd said he wanted to make up for lost time with her.

Now, she told herself again, *I'm getting what I want, what I've wanted for years—Jonathan.*

As Paris got up from her blanket in the corner of the room, came to the table and sat expectantly in front of Caroline, Graham started talking about a dog he'd had as a child, and Mary Anne let her thoughts wander, only to be interrupted by the sound of footsteps on the porch.

She cringed as the front door opened. *Let it not be awful.*

There they were, Mary Anne's father, tall and rugged-looking, a handsome devil, as Aunt Caroline had said. And her mother, tall, too, but never seeming tall. Seeming to want to be unseen.

Paris hurried to the door, tail wagging, to greet and sniff the newcomers.

Mary Anne's mother's hair had been ash-blond and now was liberally threaded with silver. It was very straight and cut short in a sort of Dorothy Hamill style, a wedge shape that had been popular around the time Mary Anne was born. She wore a lavender cardigan and blue slacks, both unobtrusive. She was bending over her plastic tote bag, looking for something and fussing.

Mary Anne's father said, "Well, hello."

Graham had stood almost the moment the door opened and Mary Anne got up, too, less gracefully, banging the edge of the table.

Mary Anne's father greeted Paris fondly. "Hi, you little mop." Then, he turned to Mary Anne to hug her and shook hands with Graham.

In these circumstances, it was her father whom Mary Anne counted on to behave like a normal person. Swiftly she made introductions, "Dad, Mom, this is Graham Corbett. He's a friend who lives down the street. Graham—Jon Clive and Katie Drew."

"Hello, Graham," they both responded.

Mary Anne's mother said, "Now, Caroline, you know Mother doesn't want your dog inside."

She sounded exactly like a scolding older sibling— actually almost like a scolding mother talking to a young child.

Mary Anne wanted to sink into the floor.

"Katie, Paris is clean and well-behaved, and Mother has let her stay here before." Caroline lingered in the doorway behind Graham and Mary Anne.

"Don't let us interrupt your dinner," Mary Anne's father said.

"I think we've just finished," Graham replied, looking at Mary Anne and Caroline for confirmation.

"Have you eaten?" Mary Anne asked her parents, wanting to look behind her to see if the wine bottle was empty and knowing it wasn't. Stupid reflex, like all the tricks of childhood she had tried to keep her father from drinking. Wine wasn't usually his tipple, yet she wanted all forms of alcohol out of his sight. She began to wonder if there was any chance he could stay sober the entire time he was in Logan. She wanted, more than anything, to call Cameron, the one person who had seen Mary Anne's father in action through most of her life, the person who really understood.

"Yes, we stopped at Shakey's," her mother replied, straightening up a bit. Straightening as if she was reminding herself to do so.

Graham sensed the tension in the air, siblings circling each other—Mary Anne's mother and her aunt. Mary Anne seemed to have turned as brittle as a thin sheet of ice. Well, families could be like this. He was an only child and had always gotten on well with his parents, but his wife's family certainly had exhibited all the ordinary drama of life.

The doorbell rang.

The caller was Paul Cureux, and Mary Anne felt color flood her face. *If he says anything about the love potion...*

Paul's hands were full of brochures. "I'm campaigning for my father."

Mary Anne said quickly, "We're voting for him, Paul. Of course, we are." She wondered if she needed to introduce him to her family. On the one hand, he was just somebody handing out election material. On the other hand, he was Cameron's special friend.

Quickly, she made introductions, adding that he was a friend of Cameron's and that his father, a neighbor, was defending his city council seat in the coming election. David Cureux had bought his house in the years since Mary Anne's parents had moved away, so they didn't know him.

Nonetheless, Mary Anne's father felt compelled to say, "Well, tell your dad we'll do all we can to talk up his campaign while we're here. Come to think of it, why doesn't Mother Billingham have a sign in her yard?" he asked his wife.

"She thinks campaign signs hurt the grass," Mary Anne said.

"Well, that's nonsense," he told his daughter. "Paul, I'll tell you what. I'll come over and pick up a sign tomorrow, and we'll get Mrs. Billingham's permission to display it. How is that?"

"Great," Paul agreed, giving Graham Corbett such a curious look that Mary Anne was sure Cameron had confided the whole story of the love potion. *Damn it, Cameron. How could you?*

Mary Anne knew how. Cameron felt rejected by Graham and was now seeing him pursue Mary Anne. She'd probably talked to Paul about it, to some degree. They *were* close friends.

And, as Mary Anne moved to shut the door behind him, Paul turned and stage-whispered, "Is it working?"

Red-faced, she closed the door without answering.

Mary Anne's mother promptly said, "Now, Jon Clive, Mother doesn't want signs in the yard. She says political views are private."

Mary Anne knew this, too, but she hadn't wanted to say it in front of Paul. And the nonsense about the grass was true as well.

Her father moved toward the living room and said, "Well, how about a drink, Mary Anne?"

She said numbly, "Help yourself," disturbed by the move, which she knew was an assertion against all Jacqueline Billingham's mores.

In proximity to both her parents, she suddenly decided that her father had an infinitely greater potential to humiliate her than her mother did. He would get drunk and chase women, and then he would apologize in a maudlin way, publicly confessing all his offenses, and swearing to do better.

Graham, thank God, was reaching for his coat. "I think I'll head home and let you enjoy seeing each other again. I'm glad your grandmother's better, Mary Anne. Nice to meet you all. Thanks for the wonderful dinner, Caroline."

"My pleasure, Graham. I'm so glad to meet you," Mary Anne's aunt said.

Mary Anne saw that Caroline already had her cigarettes and lighter in hand, and she read this as a stress reaction to the arrival of her parents.

Mary Anne stepped out onto the porch to say goodnight to Graham without closing the door behind her. If she had, her mother would have found a pretext for opening it.

Graham told her, "It's nice to meet some of your family, Mary Anne."

Her face felt stiff as she smiled, and she hoped that in the shadows of the porch light he wouldn't notice. Watching him head down the front walk to the street, she thought again about her father inside, starting his visit to Logan with a drink.

CHAPTER NINE

GRAHAM CORBETT spent Halloween afternoon raking leaves in his yard and bagging them to take to the dump. The sky was a dark gray, and the wind blew his leaves and the neighbors' yards in small tornadoes over the dry grass.

Mary Anne's father gave Graham a casual nod as he strode up David Cureux's front walk. Graham had the idea that Jon Clive Drew wasn't quite sure where he'd seen Graham before.

As Graham was loading a bag of leaves into his car—and before Mary Anne's father reached his neighbor's front door—Paul Cureux and Cameron cruised up on their mountain bikes, sweaty from a ride. Both waved to Graham, Cameron tentatively and Paul indifferently.

Graham waved back, wondering why Paul Cureux wasn't at the state park zoo, which must be open that day. Then he looked at his watch and realized it was already five-thirty, giving him only half an hour to get the leaves to the dump.

"Hello, there," Jon Clive said. "I just came by to pick up a campaign sign. Do our part for your dad, Paul."

"The grass will withstand it?" Paul asked, a bit amused.

Graham saw Cameron give him a surreptitious dig with her elbow.

"Well, considering that Mother Billingham is in the hospital, we who are in Middleburg will claim ignorance of her wishes concerning grass."

"It doesn't look like Dad's home," Paul said, climbing off his bike. "Tell you what, Mr. Drew. I'll get a sign, bring it over and put it up for you, with minimal harm to the grass."

"Why, thanks, Paul. That will do. Who's this nice-looking woman with you?"

Your niece, Graham thought, trying not to be offended by Jon Clive Drew's flirtatious tone. It was probably just his way.

But it was Cameron who seemed to be thinking along the same lines. "It's nice to see you, Uncle Jon Clive. When did you and Aunt Katie arrive?"

Graham tried not to eavesdrop on the three, but he was fascinated by everything to do with Mary Anne's family. Soon, in any case, Jon Clive Drew headed back toward Jacqueline Billingham's house, and Paul and Cameron laid their bicycles on David Cureux's lawn.

They went round into the backyard, emerging soon with a campaign poster that could be planted with an innocuous wire stand the diameter of coat hanger wire.

Graham was starting to get into his car when he heard Cameron say, "Oh, no, you don't! Paul, don't you dare tell him."

Tell who what?

To Graham's surprise, he found that both were glancing uneasily at him.

"Why not?" Paul said. "It might help your cause, and you know I always want to help you with these things, Cameron."

"Ha-ha," she said mirthlessly.

"I'm like a brother to you. I have your best interests in mind."

Now, both of them seemed determined *not* to look at Graham, and he headed to the dump and recycling center as much in the dark as before.

"Do you know how mortified Mary Anne would be if that were publicly known?" Cameron asked as she watched Graham Corbett's car disappear down the street.

"She'd get over it," Paul said. "You could just let it slip."

"*I* will never let it slip. I can't believe your mother did—to you."

"Oh, I'm sworn to secrecy. It's a family obligation," Paul said with every appearance of mischief in his face. "Of course, another plan would be for *you* to dose him with love potion."

"Your mother already told me he's all wrong for me."

Paul now looked truly shocked. "You'd do that? *You'd* do that? I mean, Mary Anne, I can see, but I thought you were more ethical."

Cameron glared at him. "Why ever should you think that? I tell approximately one person a week that I'm 'involved' with you. Don't you think that's unethical?"

"Of course not," Paul replied. "You and I have an arrangement that suits both of us and keeps us safely single—though I'm dying to know what Graham Corbett understands about our relationship."

"Well, of course, I've never told *him* I'm seeing you."

"Then, it's just as well he doesn't like you," Paul answered, "or I'd have to find a new method for preventing women from throwing themselves at me."

Cameron rolled her eyes. "Just act like yourself. That should do the trick." Then, she thought of all the unhappy relationships she'd seen in her work at the women's resource center and muttered, "Then again, maybe it would have the reverse effect."

"YOU'RE ON A SHOW about dating?" Mary Anne's mother said. "Not one of those talk shows where people tell terrible things about themselves. I think those are so tacky."

Mary Anne was glad that Graham wasn't present. No, she and her parents and Aunt Caroline were at the hospital, waiting for visiting hours to begin. It was the day of Mary Anne's second radio show with Graham, and she hadn't seen him since their dinner together. She'd told her parents she'd only be able to say hi to Nanna and then dash away. In addition to it being the day of her second radio appearance with Graham, this was election night. She would be on the radio all evening with Jonathan— with whom she'd had one date since their first night out, a date from which she'd come away with the distinct impression that he wanted to get her into bed as soon as possible. She wasn't sure why she didn't yield. She was in love with him, wasn't she?

Yes. But she wasn't sure that he was in love with her.

She told her mother, "No, the show's not like that. It's very tame."

She wasn't encouraging her family to listen to Graham's show, but Aunt Caroline said, "I'm going to make sure I'm home by the radio for that."

"Oh, yes," said Mary Anne's mother. "I want to hear it."

Mary Anne hoped the day's questions from listeners wouldn't include any about sex.

She noticed her father glancing around restlessly. She was familiar with this restlessness in him and associated it with drunkenness and ensuing chaos. He had had drinks in the evenings ever since arriving in Logan, but he'd done so at home, which tended to minimize the trouble he caused. He and Aunt Caroline and her mother played cards together, a game called Progressive Rummy, which went on for hours. Sometimes Mary Anne joined them. Twice, Aunt Louise and her husband and Cameron had come over and played, too.

Aunt Caroline was three years younger than Louise. She was the youngest and had been the prettiest. Mary Anne sometimes tried to imagine her parents and aunts and uncle in school together, her father dating first Aunt Caroline and then Mary Anne's mother. None of them seemed to like to talk about it, which Mary Anne supposed was natural. Whenever she asked basic questions— for instance, when her parents had first noticed each other—her mother said uninformative things like, "Well, we were both from Logan."

"I hope you aren't serious with that man," her mother said.

"Who?"

"The man from the radio."

Mary Anne still wasn't sure whether her mother meant Graham, whom she'd met, or Jonathan, whom she hadn't. Without bothering to narrow it down, she demanded, "What would be wrong with that?"

"Well, I think you know how your father and I feel about marriage."

In fact, Mary Anne *didn't* know. All she knew was that right now her mother was hinting at the fact that she didn't want her daughter sleeping with a man to whom she wasn't married.

Mary Anne tried to remember everything years of therapy had taught her. For instance, now was a good time to reestablish boundaries. But it didn't seem easy at the moment. She settled for saying brightly, "I don't think there's anything for you to worry about, Mom."

"Well, he seems nice," her mother said, as if doubting that this first impression was accurate, but confirming that she'd been talking about Graham Corbett.

MARY ANNE HAD ONE STOP to make before the radio station, and she was dreading it. Aunt Caroline would turn fifty-one the next day, and she'd been talking about a scarf she'd fallen in love with at the Blooming Rose, where Angie Workman worked.

Mary Anne had considered pretending that she'd never heard her aunt mention the scarf. She'd spent some time telling herself that she could find an even *more* special gift somewhere else in Logan. But this was plain old cowardice. She'd done her best to steal Jonathan Hale from Angie, and her best was proving to be pretty damned good. It had already destroyed their engagement...or so Mary Anne believed. Because no sooner had he broken up with Angie, than Jonathan had asked her out.

She blew through the door, determined to appear in a hurry, and rushed to the sale rack where Aunt Caroline had seen the scarf.

Angie emerged from the back room, her blond hair held back with barrettes in that style that was so...unimaginative. She wore a periwinkle blue suit, wrong for the season but beautiful on her. Her heels matched.

Focusing on the shoes, Mary Anne exclaimed, "I love those!"

"Thank you. We have them here." Angie's friendliness seemed to have dimmed a bit. "I love your jacket."

Mary Anne had dressed specially for the afternoon and evening. She wore her favorite buff suede pants, a dark brown silk blouse and a long dark green leather jacket.

"If I tried to wear that color, I'd look like something that should be buried," Angie said. "And, Mary Anne, I heard that your grandmother wasn't doing well. How is she now?"

Unable to keep from noticing how polite Angie was, Mary Anne gave an abbreviated medical report. "Thank you for asking," she concluded.

Angie said, "I guess you're on your way to cover election night with Jonathan."

Mary Anne wondered how Angie had known she would be doing this. "After Graham's show. I'm his 'dating expert.'"

"He seems nice," Angie said. "A friend of mine was in therapy with him for a while."

Mary Anne nodded, unable to think of anything else to say.

"Well, what can I help you find?"

But Mary Anne had already spotted the scarf Caroline had admired. "This," she said, drawing it carefully from its clip.

"That's a pretty one," Angie said. "Will you want it gift-wrapped?" With the second sense of a good salesperson, Angie seemed to know it wasn't for Mary Anne.

"Yes, please." Part of her thought it might be wiser to get out of the store before any unpleasant scene occurred. But Angie didn't seem remotely interested in making one.

Mary Anne thought that any other woman would commiserate with Angie on her broken engagement. But Mary Anne certainly couldn't do this. So she stayed silent, listening to the country music playing through the store while Angie wrapped the scarf.

Before she left, Angie said, "I hope you enjoy yourself tonight."

"Thank you," Mary Anne replied, wondering what, precisely, Angie meant. "I'll be happy if I don't make a fool of myself on the air."

CAMERON MCALLISTER was uneasy. This week's Women of Strength event was a day-long self-defense class. Cameron had taught it in conjunction with Paul, who taught tae kwon do locally and donated his time for women's self-defense classes whenever they were offered.

This class was better attended than many others in the past, attracting women beyond those who made use of the women's resource center. One of them was Angie Workman's friend Elinor Sweet, whose unlikely partner for many of the events had been Paul's sister, Bridget. Though Elinor hadn't seemed thrilled with the arrangement at first, Cameron had noticed that soon Bridget was wowing Angie's friend with talk of cosmic alignment, forces of nature, crystal energy and other New Age topics. And Cameron had been displeased to notice that part of their conversation was about Angie Workman's recently dissolved engagement.

"The soul-mate relationship," Bridget insisted, "*cannot* be broken. There's no need for anyone *ever* to mourn a breakup, because there really is no such thing between true spiritual partners."

Though Paul's opinion was that his sister did everything in her power to make herself unattractive—from not removing body hair *he* thought excessively hobbitlike to not *combing* the hair on her head—Cameron knew Bridget to be an extremely attractive woman, who'd never, to Cameron's knowledge, known rejection from any man she desired. This made her assertions about unrequited love a little hard to hear.

But Cameron didn't like the way the conversation was going because she, Cameron, had persuaded Mary Anne Drew to buy a love potion, and though that potion had never reached its intended target, its purpose had been to disrupt a soul-mate connection between Angie Workman and Jonathan Hale. And in Cameron's opinion, Bridget was no more discreet than her brother, who seemed to take a special pleasure in bringing up the subject within earshot of people who'd be fascinated to learn the facts.

Her horror increased when she heard Bridget mention love potions to Elinor. "For instance, my mother has the sight and has brewed love potions for many years, but the nature of a love potion is only to unite a soul-mate connection. Even when a love potion reaches the quote, unquote, wrong person, it is the wisdom of the potion that is acting, finding the correct place to act."

"Love potions?" Elinor said. She appeared thoughtful, as if she might be wondering whether a love potion could reunite Angie and Jonathan.

Cameron came over to the pair and said, "Okay, let's see your wrist release. Bridget, grab Elinor's wrist."

Five minutes later, Paul told Cameron none too softly, "Bridget's selling her partner on love potions."

"I don't want to talk about it," Cameron said shortly,

following the method she thought might be best for dis-couraging him. If she started blushing or showing fear, he would seize upon it as annoyingly as a playground bully.

"I think it's a worthy topic," he said.

Cameron decided to play her hole card, which was something she knew from her contact with his family. "Bridget would like to brew one for you to drink. She finds your distaste for commitment distressing and she wants her children to have little cousins to play with."

His reaction was all she'd hoped for. He shut up and shot his sister an assessing and condemnatory look. "She never would," he said, but not so much to Cameron as to the world in general. "It would go against everything my mother ever taught her."

"Except how to brew love potions," Cameron an-swered sweetly and moved away.

BEFORE SHE AND GRAHAM went on the air, while they were waiting for the show to begin, Mary Anne told him, "I like your jacket."

"Thank you." He smiled down at the rich brown blazer. "Busy with your family? I understand your grand-mother's better."

"Yes. How did you learn that?"

He nodded in the direction of Jonathan Hale. Mary Anne nodded.

Graham said, "He seems to be the source of all current news about you."

Soon they were on the air and Graham opened with the day's dating topic, Is all fair in love?

The first question seemed off-subject to Mary Anne— a breakup issue from a thirty-eight-year-old woman named Kay. "Graham, I was seeing this guy, and everything was going really well. Now, a few months ago, all of a sudden, he would hardly talk to me. He is always remote now. He suddenly doesn't have time to get together and he just says he doesn't really have time for a relationship. And no matter how many times I ask what's wrong and if I did anything to upset him, he just says nothing has changed, he's just really busy. We were good friends, and now we're not even friends.

"The thing is, I know he does this to people when he's mad at them. So, he's mad at me and he won't say why, and I have no idea what I did." As if to squeeze her question into the day's topic, she added, "He's not being fair to me."

Mary Anne watched the even breaths rising and falling in Graham's chest. She could tell from the expression in his eyes that he was focused entirely on the questioner and her question. He said, "Kay, I've known people like this. Now, I don't know you, so I don't know if you're someone who imagines people are mad at her when they're not. But you said there's been a change in your relationship, so it sounds to me as if something did happen—for him anyhow.

"All I can tell you is that if he still hasn't told you what the problem is, he probably never will. And it may never seem fair to you."

Mary Anne was making up her mind about the man who'd dumped Kay without any explanation. She interjected, "Graham, is that passive aggression?"

"Well, it can look that way if you're on the receiving end of it. But I don't think what you call it is as important as it is to accept that there are some things you can't change."

"Do you think he'll be back?"

Why would you want him? Mary Anne thought.

"Even if he does, you'll have some big communication work to do."

"Do you think he's being honest with me?"

"Kay, if he cares about you at all, he's going to be reluctant to say anything he thinks will give you pain. I'd just let this one go. Believe there's something better out there for you. I believe there is."

"Okay." She sounded forlorn. "Thank you, Graham."

"Thank you, Kay. Look in the mirror and remind yourself how special you are. Even if the man of your destiny hasn't found you yet, you can make yourself feel great. And that's something you can carry with you every day, your whole life long."

There was a gap between callers, and Mary Anne said, "Graham, did I just hear you say that we each have a destiny in regard to our romantic future? Do you think we each have a soul mate?"

"Probably a few of them. Most of us are likely to fall in love many times in our lives. The partner of our destiny is the one we choose to be with—I think of destiny as something we make happen." He gave her a smile, his eyes conveying the intimacy they had shared on their one date. The smile said he liked her, said maybe he would choose to be with her. But then his eyes shifted through the window of the booth…toward Jonathan Hale.

"We have another caller. Hello, this is Graham Corbett. You're on the air."

"Graham, my name's Elinor. This really is a question about fairness in love. What do you think about a man breaking an engagement with one woman and immediately asking another out—and her agreeing?"

Mary Anne knew immediately who the caller was. Elinor Sweet. She looked from Graham to Jonathan, who had become alert as a bird of prey. He knew the caller as well as Mary Anne did. He looked less chagrined than annoyed.

Graham said, "I would say that's a case of 'All's fair in love,' Elinor."

"What if she used unfair means to steal him from his fiancée?"

Mary Anne drew her eyebrows together. Unfair means. What did Elinor mean?

"Such as?" Graham asked.

"A love potion."

Suddenly, Mary Anne felt something like relief. This was going to make Elinor look ridiculous. Elinor, not her.

"I've never heard of a love potion that worked," Graham replied.

"Suppose it *did* work?" Elinor asked. "Would that be fair?"

Mary Anne said slowly, "Didn't someone in Arthurian legend enchant Sir Lancelot somehow? I think maybe she made herself look like someone else, though. Do you remember, Graham? It didn't work though. Lancelot broke free of the enchantment. This all seems hypothetical."

"How strange *you* should say that, Mary Anne," Elinor said. "As I have reason to think *you* bought a love potion with the intention of giving it to another woman's fiancé?"

Mary Anne was shocked. Mortified and furious. Cameron would never have told Elinor Sweet such a thing. Had Cameron told Paul everything? She didn't know what to say, and she saw numbly that both Graham and Jonathan were staring at her.

Graham said, "Elinor, I think when someone breaks an engagement there's probably a good reason. It's hard to accept, but sometimes people have second thoughts about marriage as the wedding date approaches. Thanks for your call," he said firmly, ending the discussion.

The next caller was a man named Jesse. "My question is really similar to Elinor's," he said. "But first, I'm really curious if Mary Anne bought a love potion? Mary Anne, can you answer the last caller?"

What could she say? The relief she'd felt as Graham rescued her from Elinor's accusation gave way to panic. She must lie. She *must*.

She laughed, almost scornfully. "What do you think, Jesse?"

He laughed, too, accepting this. "Okay. Silly question. My question is for both of you. What *do* you think about someone trying to steal someone else's girlfriend or fiancé? Do you think it's okay?"

Graham said, "I would say it depends on the circumstances. If a couple is living together, that's often the equivalent of a common-law marriage. I definitely wouldn't try to lure a married woman from her husband."

"I don't think a person can *steal* a boyfriend or girlfriend," Mary Anne said. "That makes it sound like the person leaving the first relationship for a second has no will in the matter."

"Good point," Graham agreed.

Was it her imagination, or was he deliberately *not* looking at Jonathan?

Jesse launched into a brief story of his own situation.

He was extremely attracted to another man's girlfriend and had let her know that if she was ever again available, he'd be interested. Graham responded that he saw nothing wrong with this.

The next caller was a man who thought that it wasn't fair for a woman to go out on a date with him three times but not be physically affectionate with him.

Mary Anne knew that if her mother was listening to the show, she would at this point turn it off. Mary Anne wasn't a talk-radio listener herself, so she could understand that. She just hoped she wasn't going to have to hear about it when she returned to Nanna's house.

But for the first time it occurred to her that her family might have heard the accusation about the love potion. The love potion, however, wouldn't upset her mother nearly so much as the idea of Mary Anne attempting to "steal" another woman's fiancé.

By the end of the show, she could feel sweat not just on her upper lip but all over her face. As soon as they were through, she grabbed her water bottle and drank from it greedily.

When they emerged from the booth, Jonathan eyed Mary Anne with equal parts curiosity and compassion. "Sorry I let Elinor through. She told me her name was Judy, and honestly I didn't recognize her voice. Are you all right?"

"I'm fine," Mary Anne said blandly.

"Where did this love-potion stuff come from?" Jonathan asked.

There it was again, and this time Mary Anne truly didn't *want* to lie. She would have liked to be able to tell both these men the truth. It was all so stupid, and love potions didn't work anyhow.

Mary Anne squinted as if puzzled. "Doesn't Dr. Cureux's ex-wife make love potions? Clare—the mid-wife? Though I can't imagine her path and Elinor's crossing. Who knows?" She thought it was a first-rate acting job and hoped this would be the end of the love-potion conversation.

Graham glanced at Mary Anne. "Busy tomorrow night?"

Jonathan Hale stared at Graham, astonished. "Are you asking her out?" he said.

"Is there some reason I shouldn't?" Graham asked.

Hale replied, "Mary Anne and I are seeing each other."

Mary Anne's face grew hot…with anger. Why did he assume that? They'd had a couple of dates. She would challenge it, but not in front of Graham.

Instead, she told Graham, "It's my aunt's birthday. We'll have some sort of celebration."

With a glance at Jonathan, Graham said, "Before Jonathan set me straight, I was hoping you'd go to the movies. They're showing *My Fair Lady* at the Old Vic." The Old Vic was Logan's refurbished theater, now used for every-thing from local plays to screenings of old movies.

"Oh, I would have loved that," Mary Anne said. Know-ing she was going to have to get the facts across to Jonathan the minute they were alone, she decided to give him a hint and said to Graham, "Would you like to join us for the birthday party?"

The moment the words were out, she regretted them. Not because of anything to do with Jonathan but because it would mean Graham spending time with her parents.

"Yes," he said. "I'd like that."

Hopefully, she added, "Though we might start dinner too early for you. Five-thirty?"

"Perfect." With a triumphant smile at Jonathan, he said, "Well. Enjoy election night," and walked out of the studio swinging his car keys.

Jonathan Hale stared at Mary Anne. "What are you doing asking him? And where's my invitation?"

"I didn't invite you," she said heatedly, remembering, as soon as she spoke, that they were going to have to be on the radio together in less than an hour. "You and I have had two dates—"

"Three," he said.

Was he counting that meal when he was still engaged to Angie?

"But," Mary Anne continued as though there had been no interruption, "I'm sorry if you felt that we had an exclusive relationship. I had no idea you thought that was the case." Her own words shocked her. *Don't I want an exclusive relationship with Jonathan Hale?*

She said, "Why did you suddenly get interested in me anyway?"

Jonathan looked less arrogant, less sure of himself. "I guess I noticed Graham being so interested in you, and I took a second look. I must have been blind before."

He sounded almost forlorn. He looked at her, seemed to be thinking many things, then abruptly changed the subject. "Let's go grab something to eat before we go on the air."

CHAPTER TEN

DURING THEIR DINNER at Logan's one Indian restaurant, Jonathan was an interesting and charming companion. Mary Anne noticed that he didn't try to run down Graham, nor did he ask about her relationship with Graham or hint again that she should invite him to Aunt Caroline's birthday dinner.

Instead, they talked about the stops they would make that evening at the political headquarters for the various local candidates—usually, this meant a restaurant or bar where the group of candidates felt welcome. In the local election, it wasn't Democrat or Republican that mattered. Rather, for the city council, several candidates seemed to be part of one group wanting particular things for the city, while another group wanted other things.

Jonathan's choices for the city council were like hers, but that was irrelevant to the evening's news. They would go where candidates and voters were, beginning half an hour before the polls closed, quizzing people on the street, the candidates, the people getting out the vote.

Mary Anne swiftly found that she and Jonathan worked well together on the air. They fell into a pattern in which she would describe the scene and then he would interview the people around them. He would hand the mic back to her, so to speak, and she would describe more of what was happening. Every hour, they did a brief check on the polls of the national elections; but in Logan it was the local race that had become hot.

Mary Anne was especially impressed by the fact that Jonathan showed no ill feelings over their earlier contretemps. Granted, if he'd become surly, it probably would have destroyed any affection she did feel for him. But many men *would* have held it against her, and it didn't seem that Jonathan did.

At nine-thirty, they reached Giuseppi's Italian Bistro, where David Cureux and three other candidates for city council were awaiting the election results. Mary Anne approached the restaurant uneasily, hoping that David Cureux wouldn't be surrounded by his family, those people who knew about the love potion and had been indiscreet with that knowledge.

There'd been no time since her show with Graham to buttonhole Cameron, but Mary Anne intended to call her first thing in the morning.

Cameron, however, was at Giuseppi's, apparently as Paul Cureux's date—or groupie, since Paul was providing live music. Paul and Cameron often used such public occasions to exhibit to all of Logan that they were a couple, even though both, to each other and to their families and closest friends, insisted they weren't. To Mary Anne, it had always seemed a circuitous way of proving that they were unavailable. Part of her had always suspected that they *were* attracted to each other but unwilling to act on it. She could imagine reasons for this. Cameron's terror of ever becoming pregnant exceeded paranoia. And Paul had an equal fear of commitment.

With dismay, Mary Anne saw that her father was also among those supporting her neighbor. No, that wasn't right—he was "supporting" the bar, flirting with Elinor Sweet, of all people, who sat at a bar stool beside him basking in the attention of a man thirty years her senior. To complete the recipe for a catastrophe, across the room, sitting with David Cureux himself, was Graham.

Mary Anne's father noticed her. She saw the brief flash of guilt, of being found out, like a small boy with his hand in the cookie jar. Then he stood up and wove between tables and other patrons to reach Mary Anne. "Here you are at work," he said, smiling and breathing Jack Daniel's fumes. He planted a kiss on her cheek.

Paul returned to the microphone, picked up his guitar and sat down on a stool. "Can't perform," he said, "without mentioning my day job. Had a little trouble *at the zoo* today. We have acquired two primates, which is a lot for a small facility like ours."

Mary Anne's father told her, "I'll probably sit in on a set with Paul a little later on. I mentioned the possibility, and he was all for it."

Right.

As Paul began a version of Simon and Garfunkel's "At the Zoo," with highly customized lyrics detailing his trouble with young monkeys, Mary Anne accepted the fact that she must introduce her father and her colleague. "Jonathan, this is my dad, Jon Clive Drew. Dad, this is Jonathan Hale."

"Glad to know you," her father said. He told Jonathan, "I'm proud of her. I always knew she'd do things with herself. Newspaper editor and radio reporter, and she was a New York magazine editor, too. For a fashion magazine. Like one of those beautiful girls in *The Devil Wears Padma*."

My God. Prada! she wanted to shriek.

"No surprise she turned out so pretty. My mother was Miss McDowell County."

Shut up, Mary Anne thought. *Go away. Please go away.*

Jonathan said, "I think she's very special, too."

Mary Anne did not relax.

"She always has guys after her," her father went on. "Always been that way. It's because she's a real lady, like her mother. Really ladylike. That's how we raised her."

Mary Anne murmured to Jonathan, "Let me dash to the ladies' room before we start."

"Sure," he said, continuing to look askance at her father.

Just don't let him get started on mining. Yes, her father had left West Virginia and become a movie star. But he still loved to expand the one summer he'd spent working in the coal mines to make it sound like a lifetime of danger. After hinting at extreme risks and gory accidents, he would recount the practical jokes he and the other miners had played on each other, jokes of profound insipidity, none of which Mary Anne found funny. Replacing the filling of someone's sandwich with axle grease…gluing someone's boot to the ceiling of the dry room. Stupid, stupid, stupid. *Then* he would demand the attention of the room, borrow the nearest guitar—even if someone had to run half a mile to get it—and perform "Dark as a Dungeon." He would follow this up with a maudlin story about a man he'd barely known being crushed in a mine. And then he'd cry.

In the bathroom Mary Anne lingered, hoping that her father would return to Elinor Sweet's side. And she thought about what a terrible and selfish hope that was, that he would be lecherous toward a young woman and unfaithful to her mother—that she would have him do that rather than embarrass her with Jonathan. Inevitably, her disloyalty to her mother made her hate herself.

And loathe her father.

As she emerged at last from the ladies' room, she collided with Graham, who was leaving the men's. "Hi, there," he said.

There was a look of concern in his eyes.

Though Jonathan had been polite to her father, here, suddenly, she saw rationality; saw the serious reaction that her father's behavior merited. Here, she suddenly knew, was someone who could understand how she felt at this moment.

The knowledge shocked her. It was like an electric current, this sudden understanding of Graham Corbett's maturity and insight.

"Hi," she answered.

She thought she could hear her father's voice from the bar. She and Jonathan wouldn't be here long, and that was the only bright spot. By the time her father pushed his way to Paul's microphone, she would be elsewhere.

Graham gazed into her eyes for a long moment, looking as if he wanted to ask what he could do to help. "We had the radio on," he said at last. "You sound good."

"Thank you."

"Man, I've seen waves higher than that building across the street," came her dad's voice from the next room, louder than Paul's singing.

Mary Anne drew a slight breath of relief. Her father was onto his favorite hobby, deep-sea fishing. She found the fishing stories marginally better than mining tales. Giving Graham a small wave, she turned back toward the bar. And now she found herself face-to-face with Elinor Sweet.

Elinor said, "Nice *lie* on the radio, Mary Anne." She lifted her eyebrows at Graham. "She bought a love potion to give to Jonathan Hale. Well, no one has said who it was for, but she definitely bought one. Bridget Cureux told me."

Mary Anne was shocked at Bridget's indiscretion. She'd suspected something of the kind, suspected Paul because of his teasing. But suspicion was somehow so different from discovering that one's suspicions were true.

"I didn't lie," Mary Anne said, because she hadn't. She'd deliberately *misled* everyone, which was different.

"You've wanted him for years. He used to joke about it to Angie."

Mary Anne felt her face flood with color. Jonathan had known? And joked to his fiancée about her crush on him?

"Well, now he knows how he got interested in you. I just told him, and, believe me, he knows I'm not lying. I told him he could ask Paul Cureux if he didn't believe me."

Mary Anne's opinion of Angie Workman sank. How could she be friends with this horrible woman?

She tried to summon something resembling poise. "Whatever, Elinor. I need to get back to work." She couldn't stand to look at Graham, and only stepped around Elinor and walked back into the bar.

WITH PAUL'S MUSIC in the background, Jonathan and Mary Anne conducted their broadcast. Jonathan said, "Dr. Cureux, we're hearing from voters that their first interest is fiscal responsibility. A number of them think you can offer that, but some are concerned about past actions of members of the city council. What do you plan to do to prevent the things we've seen happen this fall?"

"You're referring to unauthorized spending on the part of individual council members," David Cureux remarked. "Jonathan, I think the democratic process is taking care of that problem. The council member involved in the problem was asked to step down and did so. The people of Logan *do* know what they want."

Mary Anne's father crowded toward the group around the microphones, leaning in around Paul Cureux's shoulder. "And we want David Cureux!" he shouted and followed this with a West Virginia University football cheer that was taken up by a few other drunks in the bar but no one else as it was entirely irrelevant to the election.

Save this, Mary Anne, she thought. *You can rescue this situation; you can avert total disaster.*

All the panicked thoughts of her youth bombarded her, telling her she could not afford to freeze now, that she *must* divert attention from her father. She said, "Dr. Cureux, I've been noticing the symbol on all your campaign posters, the family. Can you tell us about that?"

"My daughter Bridget did that. She chose to make the family out of PlaySkool figures to reinforce our belief that Logan is a good place to raise children—that it's child-friendly and that we care about kids here. Most every decision in government can be boiled down to, 'What is good for our kids?'"

"That's right, kids are everything," Jon Clive Drew said, butting in.

Mary Anne hadn't known that Bridget designed the logo. She hadn't known Bridget was capable of anything but shooting off her mouth to people like Elinor Sweet.

She saw Graham put his hand on Jon Clive's shoulder, lean close and say something to him.

Jon Clive looked up distractedly. "Progressive Rummy?"

"I met your wife and sister-in-law walking a short time ago," Graham told him. "They mentioned it. We're counting on you."

Mary Anne was fascinated by this assertion of Graham's. Could it be true? Had he gone home after his show and met her mother and aunt? How else would he know about their obsession with that card game?

Yet she couldn't help wondering if drawing her father toward home was Graham's own impulse. She wanted to know more, and she saw with disbelief and pleasure that her father was following the younger man's lead.

Her eyes suddenly streamed. Gratitude, pure and deep, shot through her. She felt that no one in her life had ever shown her more mercy than Graham Corbett had in that moment.

Outside later, as she and Jonathan put their equipment into Jonathan's car, he said, "So. Elinor gave me the lowdown on the love potion."

Mary Anne had almost missed many of her cues in Giuseppi's because she'd been planning for this conversation. She found she cared little about Jonathan's opinion at the moment, and this helped her care less about her pride. As he shut the tailgate of his Subaru station wagon, she looked at him.

She managed a small smile. "You believe that I dosed you with a love potion and that you are attracted to me because of it," she said, as if to clarify his point of view.

"Elinor encouraged me to ask Paul Cureux for the facts."

"And did you?"

"Didn't have a chance."

Mary Anne nodded. "Well, I can promise you one thing, Jonathan. I have no knowledge of you drinking any love potion."

He looked as if he didn't quite believe her.

"Do you believe yourself to be under the spell of a love potion?" she asked, taking care to sound properly amused.

Suddenly, he grinned. "Very nearly. How did Elinor come up with this story?"

"Why didn't you ask her?"

"She said it was from Bridget Cureux and that Bridget's mother made the potions."

"Yes, well, Elinor also told *me* that you used to tell your fiancée all about the crush I had on you." Mary Anne made it sound as though she found *this* unbelievable. The thing was...she didn't.

"There's some truth in that," Jonathan admitted. "I thought you liked me. I apologize if that assumption was wrong."

His honesty disarmed her. She felt it deserved an equal show of probity.

He unlocked the passenger door for her, and Mary Anne climbed in. When he had slid behind the steering wheel, she said, "I *did* buy a love potion. But I didn't give it to you."

"You gave it to someone else?" He gazed at her in amazement.

She nodded pleasantly, trying to look unconcerned.

"Did it work?" he asked. "Why did you do this?"

"For experimental purposes. And I don't believe it had any effect at all."

"Was the person supposed to fall in love with you?"

Mary Anne thought of Cameron, reminded herself that Cameron seemed to have told no one that Graham actually drank the love potion. But wasn't it Cameron's fault that Paul had found out about the potion? Cameron had explained that it was Clare who'd let the cat out of the bag to her son—or something like that. *Tomorrow I'll find out everything from her,* she told herself again.

She told Jonathan, "No. Definitely not." Because Graham Corbett had drunk the love potion. She hadn't wanted Graham to fall in love with her. She'd wanted Jonathan.

And she supposed she had him—or could if she wanted.

But all she could think about was Graham getting her father out of Giuseppi's before he could "sit in on a set" with Paul.

She thought no one had ever done anything nicer for her.

"WHAT WAS BRIDGET DOING telling Elinor Sweet all of that?" Mary Anne demanded of Cameron the next morning. She had called her cousin at nine, as early as seemed reasonable on a weekend morning.

"I think she's mad at Paul."

"Who?" Mary Anne demanded. "And what does that have to do with anything?"

"Bridget's sometimes a little passive-aggressive. She and Paul had a problem at the zoo. At least, he thinks that's what she got mad about. And it's just like her to get mad at Paul and *accidentally* let slip something that would be a problem for him."

"It didn't have anything to do with Paul! Or with Bridget."

"Well, it was supposed to get me angry at Paul, I think. I know it's all a little convoluted."

"What was the fight at the zoo about?" Mary Anne asked, accepting that Bridget's excuse for indiscretion was no excuse at all.

"She was there with the preschool group on Halloween, and Nicky, that's her son, was beside the duck pond, and she was twenty feet away talking to another mother."

"That's dangerous," Mary Anne agreed.

"Well, exactly," Cameron said. "I mean, he's just three, and the pond's four feet deep, and even if it wasn't... But Paul wasn't very tactful, I guess. He said something about her needing to stop trying to be the Mother Goddess and just try to be an adequate mother."

Mary Anne made a small sound, indicating that indeed Paul had not been tactful. "Well, at least you haven't told anybody about Graham getting the potion."

"Would I?" Cameron demanded.

"No," Mary Anne admitted. "I'm sorry."

"You're falling for him, aren't you?" said Cameron.

"For who?"

"For Graham."

Honesty warred with tact. Finally, Mary Anne said, "You know what he did last night?" And she described Graham getting her drunken father out of the restaurant.

"So Jonathan's lost his charm," Cameron said, in a tone that implied that Mary Anne was fickle, childish, impulsive, casually shifting her affections from one man to another.

"You *said* it was okay if I went out with Graham," Mary Anne told her.

"After you'd already told him you'd go out with him."

Mary Anne tried to remember if this was true and she thought it might be. "I'm sorry if I've hurt you, Cameron."

"You haven't," Cameron said, a bit coolly. "Anyhow, I'll see you tonight at the birthday party."

Which Graham would be attending—as Mary Anne's guest.

MARY ANNE'S FATHER was remorseful about his night out, and she didn't want to hear it. At the breakfast table, where he arrived at eleven, he said, "Hope I didn't embarrass you last night, Mary Anne."

She was grabbing a quick cup of coffee before heading off to a D.A.R. luncheon she was covering for the newspaper. She said nothing. There was nothing *to* say. Of course, he'd embarrassed her. Of course, she wished he wouldn't drink. She burst out, "I thought you were going to AA."

"Not anymore." He shook his head. "Those are career alcoholics there. Career *recovered* alcoholics I should say. Can't go on with their lives, those folks. No, I face up to God with my mistakes."

And keep making them, Mary Anne thought bitterly. She said, "It seems to me that people who go to AA are trying to do something difficult and they recognize they need help. And, yes, you embarrassed me."

"Damn," he said, gazing into his own cup of milky coffee. "If the Lord would only forgive me..."

Mary Anne wanted to tell him he shouldn't doubt anyone's forgiveness except the humans he'd offended.

"Where's Mom?" she asked.

"She's upstairs with your aunt, making some changes to Nanna's bedroom."

"No, she's not. She and your aunt are right here,

chicken." said Aunt Caroline, from the foot of the staircase. "Pretty suit, Mary Anne," she added, admiring the earth-toned shantung silk Mary Anne had put on for the luncheon. "I like that!" she enthused.

Thank God for Aunt Caroline. Talking of clothes, so Mary Anne wouldn't have to listen to her father's mawkish expressions of regret. Soon, he would start saying he hadn't been much of a father to her. He might even weep.

"Heard you and your Graham on the radio yesterday," Aunt Caroline said. "You two do a good job together."

Mary Anne's mother said. "I wish you wouldn't take part in those shows, Mary Anne. All those talk shows are so *tawdry*, with all those people calling up and talking about their problems. And all those questions about sex. I don't care to hear them."

"Then, you should turn off the radio," Mary Anne said matter-of-factly.

"And what was that silliness about a love potion?"

"No idea," Mary Anne answered, but was startled by the speculative look in Aunt Caroline's eyes. Cameron had visited alone with Aunt Caroline, but surely Cameron wouldn't have said... Cameron had denied mentioning it to *anyone*. "Happy birthday, Aunt Caroline," Mary Anne finally said. "Graham's going to join us for dinner."

"Wonderful," her aunt replied. "That will be such fun. Now, what shall we have? Lucille's coming to cook, and she has a few options planned. What does Graham like?"

"It's not Graham's birthday," Mary Anne replied with a smile.

"He stayed till eleven last night," her father said, "but he wouldn't stay till the end of the game."

So they *had* played Progressive Rummy.

"Very nice of him," Aunt Caroline said, and Mary Anne knew that her aunt had recognized Graham's chivalry in getting Jon Clive Drew out of the public eye.

"I wish Mother could be here with us," her aunt added. "We'll all have to go in a crowd to visiting hours and celebrate with her there."

"Now, Mary Anne," her mother said, "you know Nanna wouldn't want you being on a show like that."

Mary Anne wanted to scream. But being a lady meant not screaming even when people made you feel insane. It meant not shaking people you wanted to shake. She said, "I'm off to the luncheon. See you this afternoon. You and Mom can decide on the food with Lucille," she told Aunt Caroline.

And fled.

GRAHAM WAS LOOKING forward to the birthday party for Mary Anne's aunt. He'd observed her misery the night before and was glad, for her sake, that her father had agreed to go home to a card game. Graham spent a good part of every day now thinking about Mary Anne. She was distracting him from his professional project, that first self-help book.

Had he ever not thought her pretty? No. He'd always admired her prominent cheekbones, her incredibly lush eyelashes and eyebrows, and those green eyes. For a while, he *had* told himself she was a little heavy. But that was before he'd started admiring her posture and the natural grace with which she moved.

That had been quite a scene in the corridor outside the bathrooms the night before, with Elinor Sweet accusing Mary Anne of trying to entrap Hale with a love potion.

Once he'd heard Elinor's accusation at Giuseppi's, he seemed to remember something about a local woman making love potions—love potions some people said worked. But he'd never put it together, that the witch in question was David Cureux's ex-wife. It would be interesting to quiz David about it sometime. His neighbor, who had retained his city council seat, was a rational man, and Graham was sure that David Cureux would feel as he himself did about love potions. That they were a lot of nonsense.

Anyhow, though Jonathan Hale certainly seemed to be pursuing Mary Anne, Graham didn't suspect the station manager of being in love with her. But he was beginning to suspect himself of having certain feelings. Not in love. No. He was just attracted, very attracted. And, he told himself, he was more interested in her depth, in her personal qualities, than Hale was.

At five twenty-five in the afternoon, he left the house and walked to Mary Anne's bearing a potted begonia, wrapped in cellophane as protection from the cold. He also had a bag of dog treats that had been baked locally. The plant was for Caroline and the treats were for her dog. He'd considered bringing a bottle of wine, but then he'd thought of Mary Anne's father and decided not to.

He had only just rung the doorbell when Lucille opened the front door. She beamed her usual welcoming smile. "Well, hello, Mr. Graham. How nice you look."

"Thank you, Lucille."

Caroline called from the living room, "Hi, Graham! We're all in here."

Mary Anne, however, came to the arch that led into the

living room. She wore a gold-colored dress that hugged her shape nicely.

"You're beautiful," he said appreciatively.

"Thank you. You, too."

He sensed a tension beneath the words, a tension that stiffened her face even as she smiled at him.

He came into the living room, where Paris lay at Caroline's feet. Approaching Mary Anne's aunt, he said, "Happy birthday."

"Why, thank you! How nice. Isn't this pretty, and you remembered Paris, too."

A few feet from her sister on the sofa sat Mary Anne's mother, her mouth slightly pinched, while Jon Clive Drew stood by the sideboard. "We're having cocktails. What can I get you, Graham?"

A swift survey of the room showed that only Caroline and Jon Clive were having cocktails—a glass of wine in her case and something mixed in his. Mary Anne and her mother were drinking ice water, each with a slice of lemon.

"I'd love a glass of water," Graham said. "Some days I just don't drink enough."

Mary Anne said, "I'll get it," but Lucille shook her head and hurried toward the kitchen.

Graham asked, "How is your grandmother?"

"Fit as a fiddle," Mary Anne's father replied on her behalf. "Ready to come home and tell everyone what to do. She must know the dog's lying on the living-room carpet."

"She does know," Mary Anne's mother said. "She says she has asked Caroline not to bring Paris onto the carpeted areas."

"And Caroline has told her," Caroline replied placidly, "that Paris's little paws are cleaner than the soles of her shoes." She changed the subject. "Graham, I enjoyed listening to you and Mary Anne on your show."

For some reason, Mary Anne looked apprehensive.

"Yes, well," said Mary Anne's mother. "I think we should talk about something else."

Graham wondered why she thought so. He certainly had no intention of sitting around discussing his own radio show, but it seemed a strange remark for Mrs. Drew to make.

He had wanted to tell Caroline that Mary Anne was a great guest and that her presence filled out many discussions, but after Mrs. Drew's comment all he felt he could do was tell Caroline, "Thank you. It was nice of you to listen."

Mrs. Drew offered an explanation for which no one had asked. "I just don't like hearing all those people talk about all sorts of things. I'd rather not know."

What a telling statement, he thought, unable to keep from wondering if it extended to her own life.

Mortified by her mother's rudeness, though she knew Katie Drew would be upset to think that she'd been rude, Mary Anne said, "I'm not sure any of us is ever that lucky. What some people manage to do is to pretend that they don't know, which isn't the same thing."

A puzzled look briefly crossed her mother's face. Then, she said, "Well, Mary Anne, it's just not necessary to talk about everything in our lives."

It occurred to Graham that Mrs. Drew's response seemed almost generational—but of her mother's generation. Because once no one *had* discussed uncomfortable things—or so he sometimes thought.

Caroline rose from the couch. "I need a cigarette. I'm

going to take Paris around the block. Anyone want to come?"

"I do," Mary Anne said quickly. "Graham?"

"Wonderful," he agreed.

"Now, don't drop your cigarette butts in the neighborhood," Mrs. Drew said.

Graham couldn't imagine Mary Anne's aunt doing such a thing. In any case, she completely ignored the admonition and merely went to retrieve the Maltese's lead.

"I wonder if we should go, too," Mrs. Drew said softly to her husband.

"We'd love the company," Graham said, which was a lie. He knew that Mary Anne's eagerness to walk the dog was connected to the fact that it offered escape from her parents.

"Sure. Why not?" said Mary Anne's father.

"Well, let me see if Lucille needs my help first," said Mrs. Drew.

"Oh, hell," Mary Anne said suddenly. "I forgot. Cameron and Aunt Louise are coming. I should stay."

"I'll stay with you," Graham said. Maybe Mary Anne's parents would go with Caroline.

"Well, I'm going with Caroline and the dog," Jon Clive Drew announced, downing the remainder of whatever had been in his glass.

"Mom, you go, too," Mary Anne urged.

"Oh—shouldn't I be here for Louise?"

"Graham and I will entertain them till you get back."

"All right, then."

The dog walkers began pulling on coats, Katie Drew saying, "I wish you'd quit those things, Caroline. They're so bad for you."

Graham followed Mary Anne into the kitchen and asked Lucille, "How can we help? Set the table?"

"You absolutely may not set the table, Mr. Graham, or do one other little thing."

Graham grinned.

"And that counts for you, too, Miss Mary Anne," added Lucille. "You two go sit in the living room so you hear Miss Cameron when she arrives."

As they wandered back toward the living room, Mary Anne said, "As if she isn't going to insist on getting the door, too."

"She's a lovely person," Graham said.

"I think so, too. I just love her. When I was little, she would put *extra* butter in the brownies. It's been hard talking her out of that in the interest of remaining halfway svelte."

Graham teased, "I like how she manages you. I'm watching carefully and taking notes."

Mary Anne glanced at him in surprise. How could he want anything to do with her after her family's displays of the past twenty-four hours? She said, "You mean you're not scared off by a dysfunctional family of origin?"

He smiled at her and said, "They're very nice, Mary Anne."

What manners, was all she could think.

Taking advantage of a breather before the next bit of drama, she sank down on the couch and exhaled, relaxing every muscle in her body.

Ruefully, Mary Anne recalled the one time a man *had* asked her to marry him. A man who had never met her parents, her aunt or her grandmother. When Mary Anne had learned of dubious behavior on his part, regarding his parents' finances, she had broken the engagement. The incident had left her wondering if she was only capable of securing someone defective; if men could somehow *sense* that she came from a screwy family and if they gave her what they thought she deserved.

She tried to make a joke. "Did he sing 'Dark as a Dungeon' on the way home last night?"

Graham shook his head, smiling fondly and, he hoped, sympathetically.

"How did he get there, anyway?" she asked.

"What I picked up when we got back here," he said, "is that he set out for a solo walk and didn't return and everyone guessed he'd gone to a bar."

Mary Anne stirred at the sound of an automobile on the street. She peered out the window to see the taillights of a large sedan that was pulling up to the curb. "That will be Cameron and Aunt Louise."

And Cameron was mad at her. And she was a little mad at Cameron for involving her with the Cureux family.

Mary Anne beat Lucille to the door by two steps. She welcomed Cameron and her mother into the foyer, helping her aunt off with her coat as Cameron brandished a rolled-up magazine. "A present for you, Mary Anne. From Paul. He says he's going to recommend his mother use it for advertising."

Mary Anne held a finger to her lips and mouthed, "No! No!"

A look of incredulity crossed Cameron's face. Casually, she glanced into the living room and waved to Graham.

To Mary Anne, it all seemed dreadfully obvious and damning.

"Well, here." Cameron thrust the magazine into Mary Anne's hands.

It was the weekly entertainment news magazine *Fly*. "Why is it called that?" she asked Cameron.

"Fly," Cameron said. "You know, like they used to say in England during the Napoleonic Wars. It means, like, really good in every way. I dog-eared the page. Graham can see it, too."

Mary Anne opened the magazine and saw the photo the *Logan Standard* junior reporter had snapped of her and Graham on their evening out.

Horror washed over her. Graham looked handsome, like a movie star. Her hips looked like something that should be labeled Wide Load. The worst thing was the caption. *Dr. Graham Corbett steps out with Jon Clive Drew's daughter, Mary Anne.*

She wanted to sit down.

Cameron grabbed the magazine from her hand and took it into the living room.

Mary Anne felt as if she'd been photographed walking down the street in her nightgown. It was in no sense a rational reaction and had everything to do with the tabloid features involving her father she'd come across when she was young.

She followed her cousin into the living room, walked to the sideboard and poured herself a glass of wine.

Graham said, "You're photogenic, Mary Anne."

"You want some wine?" she answered without enthusiasm.

"I'm fine."

Lucille popped into the living room and said she was brewing "a nice pot of tea," then continued to offer various refreshments.

Aunt Louise said, "Is Caroline out smoking?"

"Walking Paris with my parents." Mary Anne looked uneasily at Cameron, who was prowling the living room looking irritable.

Soon Aunt Louise and Graham were talking about Graham's mother's books, a discussion that continued as the others returned from dog-walking. Aunt Louise called out, "Caroline, did you know Graham's mother is Evelyn Corbett?"

"Yes, I told him *Sultry Southern Custom* is my favorite!" Aunt Caroline exclaimed.

Mary Anne's mother looked shocked. "It sounds terrible," she murmured audibly.

Louise, falling into family step, said, "Well, our mother won't read anything like that."

Mary Anne was certain that Aunt Caroline had mentioned that very title so as to provoke a reaction from her sisters. She seemed to sometimes enjoy making them appear gauche.

Mary Anne managed to say, "I'm sure we all agree that it's an amazing feat to have become such a well-known and much-loved author."

Her mother took her cue at once and said, "It certainly is."

"Graham's working on a book, too," Mary Anne said, though he had only spoken of it once in her presence— to Jonathan. "It's sort of like his show, I guess. Self-help. And he helps a lot of people," she added with a meaningful look at her mother.

Which was the cue for her father, who'd been hanging up his coat, to enter the room and say, "Cameron McAllister, look at you. My niece is a *fox*."

Mary Anne considered simply walking out of the house and never returning.

Jon Clive waved to Louise, saying, "No Skip?"

"He's got a meeting tonight."

Mary Anne's father helped himself to another drink, saying, "Graham, can I tempt you?"

"Not just now, thanks."

Cameron leaped up from the couch. "Ready to open a present, Aunt Caroline?"

"I'm always ready for that, chicken." Aunt Caroline laughed. "I don't want to interfere with Lucille's plans, though."

Mary Anne said, "I'll ask when we're eating." While she was in the kitchen, maybe she could put her head in the oven. She ducked through the dining room to the kitchen, where she let out a long breath.

Lucille saw her face and said, "Miss Mary Anne, nothing any other person on earth does can reflect on you. You're the only one who can do that."

Mary Anne came over to the black woman and clung to her for a moment. Lucille was almost as tall as she was. Mary Anne was so grateful for her voice of sanity in this time of chaos.

Lucille said, "Now, your aunt's going to want a bottle of wine on the table. She already said so."

Mary Anne had overheard Aunt Caroline saying so. *Lucille, I'm not going to let that man's bad behavior ruin my birthday. Nobody will keep him away from the side- board anyhow.*

"When shall we eat?" Mary Anne asked.

"Fifteen minutes, if that works for everyone."

"Thank you so much, Lucille. Won't you let me do *anything*?"

"You know better than to ask that, Miss Mary Anne."

Mary Anne returned to the living room, where Aunt Caroline sat unwrapping the gift Cameron and Aunt Louise had brought. It turned out to be a gorgeous silver bowl. "How *beautiful!*" Aunt Caroline exclaimed. "You shouldn't have, but I am *so glad* you did."

Mary Anne smiled, thinking of her own gift for her aunt, the scarf that had been gift-wrapped by Angie Workman, sitting in its box on a side table in the dining room.

Mary Anne told everyone when dinner would be served and Aunt Caroline opened another present, this one from Mary Anne's parents. It was a white cotton sweater, very nice, well-suited to Caroline's style. Lucille came out to announce dinner, and Mary Anne and the others trailed into the dining room, where an extra leaf had been added to the table to accommodate the crowd. Her father brought his whiskey glass with him, and Mary Anne wondered why Lucille had bothered to mention the wine, which was now breathing on the table. As Lucille served the ham, Louise said, "Caroline, you know who I saw yesterday? Dean Milligan! Remember that night we all went to the drive-in to see *Jaws?*"

"I remember that," said Mary Anne's father. "You were wearing that green sweater, Caroline, and hip-huggers, the first time they came around, and, boy, did you have the hips for them."

"You weren't there, Jon Clive," said Louise, frowning. "Were you?"

Mary Anne realized this was probably a date her father

had gone on with her aunt before he switched to her mother. She barely stopped herself from rolling her eyes.

"I never saw that movie," Katherine Drew said. "Mother didn't approve of it. I remember that."

Aunt Caroline said, "Graham, are you going to pour that wine for us?"

"I am," Graham said swiftly, standing up to do so.

Louise said, "I'm so silly, Caroline. It was Sue Lane who went with us. I don't know why I thought it was you."

"Probably," Mary Anne said, "because she went out with my father before my mother did." She smiled at Graham as she said this.

"Well, I'm surprised Louise went to that movie!" her mother exclaimed. "Knowing how Mother felt about it."

Across the table, Cameron uncapped a small vial and added the clear contents to her own wineglass, then picked up the glass and drank.

Mary Anne's mouth fell open, and it was all she could do not to shout out, "What are you doing?"

Because the vial was identical to the one Clare Cureux had given her, the vial containing the love potion.

CHAPTER ELEVEN

MARY ANNE FOLLOWED her cousin to the bathroom fifteen minutes later, pushing her way into the tiny powder room with Cameron. "What was that—the vial? At dinner?"

Cameron tossed her long braids and shrugged. "Not a love potion. Don't worry. I asked Bridget for something to help me realign emotionally."

"What do you mean?" Mary Anne gazed into her cousin's dark eyes, feeling terrible for the pain she saw there.

"You're going to end up with Graham," Cameron said. "And it's *okay*. It's really okay. He has never been interested in me. But Bridget just brewed up something to help me adjust, to help me come back to myself emotionally."

"I wouldn't drink anything anyone in that family gave me," Mary Anne said, suddenly thinking it had been a terrible thing to plan to give a man a love potion. "I wouldn't do business with them, especially not with *her*. Don't you think she'll tell everyone all about it?"

"Actually, no," Cameron answered. "We discussed it all. I was mad at her for what she said to Elinor and I told her so, told her everything I thought. She said I was right and apologized. She *admitted culpability*. She's really not so bad."

"So, does she supposedly have her mother's supposed powers?"

"Oh, yes. Even Paul admits that she does. He just says she shouldn't use them."

Mary Anne sighed and abruptly put her arms around her much smaller cousin. "I'm sorry, Cameron. I'm sorry for everything."

"Hell, Mary Anne, it doesn't matter." Cameron turned away for a moment, but Mary Anne knew it was to hide tears. "This thing with Graham. I mean, *you're* my best friend. Like I'm going to get along without you. Give me a break."

Mary Anne returned to the table acutely thankful for the love of her cousin. Cameron's nature was forgiving. *I hope she gets over Graham fast.*

Strangely, their brief conversation had made her feel free, and she found herself looking across the table at Graham with new eyes.

But he's a celebrity, Mary Anne. You're in that stupid magazine together.

But what had they been doing? Going on a date. No setting fire to bars, no epic car chases, no drunken scenes with multiple strippers.

I can live with it, she thought, watching Graham converse with her mother about her job as church secretary. Everything was changing. She realized abruptly that she was not in love with Jonathan Hale and didn't care if they ever had another date.

The person she cared about was Graham Corbett.

AFTER DESSERT, as they sat in the living room with Cameron and Aunt Caroline, Graham said, "Mary Anne, this is going to sound silly, but I was hoping you'd come over and look at some furniture catalogs with me. My mother's coming for Thanksgiving, and I need to pick out some things for the guest room."

Cameron, who had been steadily consuming merlot on top of Bridget's love cure, said, "You don't have an insect collection you want her to see?"

Mary Anne couldn't help it. She burst out laughing. So did Graham.

Aunt Caroline just shook her head and grabbed her cigarettes, perhaps planning to step outside.

Mary Anne said, "I'd love to help you pick out furniture, Graham."

Cameron pulled out her cell phone, which had been vibrating in her pocket, and answered it. After initial greetings, Mary Anne heard her say, "Paul, I don't *want* to be a groupie tonight. Just tell her you have a girlfriend, and she'll go away. Anyhow, I can't drive. I'm too drunk." A sigh. "Jake is coming to get me? Oh, God. Tell him I'll meet him at the bridge."

Apparently, Cameron couldn't stand the thought of family introductions.

"You're going to owe me *big*-time," Cameron told her non-boyfriend.

Graham stood and lifted his eyebrows, tilting his head toward the foyer.

"OH, THANK GOD," Mary Anne said when they hit the street. "And thank *you*."

He smiled. "I spent a good bit of time coming up with a pretext to get you over to my house, though your cousin saw right through it."

"She's very perceptive."

"With all your family at your grandmother's house, I figured this was the time to tempt you with the peace of my place. Maybe I can dissuade you from going back."

Mary Anne laughed and also felt a delicious tingling in her stomach, spreading through her whole body. She glanced up at Graham in the streetlight, to try to gauge how serious he was.

Just flirting, she decided. But she said, "It was kind of you to take my father home last night."

"I enjoyed his company," Graham told her.

That couldn't be true, but Mary Anne appreciated the words.

He said, "There's a concert next weekend in Charleston. A little-known blues artist, but I've heard him before and I like him. Interested?"

"I'd like that. Thank you." Obviously he realized that she and Jonathan were *not* seeing each other, not in the exclusive way Jonathan had implied.

"Good," Graham answered. "I'm glad I didn't have to foist the tickets on someone else."

He glanced over at her, loving her profile, wanting to touch those thick, dark eyebrows and eyelashes, her full upper lip. In a back corner of his mind, he thought of Briony and what had happened to him after her death. Surely he could have a few dates with Mary Anne without falling head over heels in love with her. Attachment to her didn't have to be as strong as it had been between him and his wife.

Mary Anne laughed suddenly, and he looked at her.

She said, "I can't *wait* till they all go home."

"Your family?"

"Yes."

"I've got a place you can stay," he offered with a grin.

"That would probably cause a family crisis."

They both laughed, and as they walked up the front steps Graham said, "Care for coffee or something stronger while we pore over those furniture catalogs?"

Mary Anne asked, "*Are* there furniture catalogs?"

"Of course, but if you'd rather let me beat you at chess again…"

"I'm a world champion furniture shopper," Mary Anne replied.

HE REALLY DID HAVE a spare room that he wanted to furnish for his mother's visit. There were already filmy white curtains covering insulated blinds. There was also a single bed covered only with a mattress pad, about which Graham said, "This is going to charity. David Cureux has already asked me if I had anything to donate."

"He's a nice man," Mary Anne remarked, flipping through one of the catalogs they'd brought upstairs.

Graham sat down on the bed beside her, right next to her, and looked at her curiously. "So tell me all about this love potion. Is it a figment of Elinor Sweet's imagination?"

The tension the topic produced warred with the effect of his closeness. *How did I ever fail to notice how sexy this man is?* She hardly knew how to answer.

How about the truth, Mary Anne?

She took the general tack she had taken with Jonathan. "There *was* a love potion. It was something Cameron and I did just for fun. But I *didn't* give it to Jonathan Hale."

"Did you give it to someone else?"

Mary Anne silently gave thanks for how he'd phrased

the question. She *hadn't* given him the love potion. He'd seized it. "No, I didn't."

"What did you do with it?"

She closed her mouth, considered. "There was an accident." She looked up at him and made herself grin. "I promise I will tell you about it someday."

"Someday?" He seemed delighted with this answer, and abruptly he brought his mouth near hers and kissed her lips.

Everything warm and wanting surged through her, as if a tide within her swept toward him, unstoppable. It felt so good to kiss him.

When he pulled away, pulled just two inches away, it was to say, "I've been wanting to do that for ages."

"Ages?" she asked skeptically.

"Probably since I first laid eyes on you. Though I argued with myself about it for a long time."

"Why?"

"It was pretty obvious you didn't like me and that you were hot for Hale."

She blushed. "You're not the first person to observe that last part." She was unaccountably nervous, but also extremely attracted to him. She found herself saying, "You know, I never even knew you'd been married until that night you came over."

He said nothing, and Mary Anne looked into his brown eyes. He seemed on the verge of speaking.

When he said nothing, she told him, "Jonathan said you went through a bad time after your wife died."

Graham nodded, biting his bottom lip. "Yes. It was the worst thing that had ever happened to me. Not just her dying. But afterward. I almost destroyed my life. I believed nothing mattered and I acted that way." He stared into space as he said, "Sometimes you have to almost lose everything you have to learn what it's worth."

"I hope I never have to find out that way," Mary Anne told him.

"Is there a chance in the world," he said, "that I could talk you into spending the night?"

Mary Anne knew the answer, knew it in her soul. Strangely, the short time she'd spent dating Graham had begun to feel like the most mature relationship of her life so far. And the best.

IN THE MOONLIGHT, Graham watched her sleep. God, she was beautiful. He'd been unprepared for the impact of those eyes of hers on his as they made love. It was as if they were seeing inside each other.

He *was* in love with her. He hadn't wanted to be, hadn't wanted to love any woman this way. It felt more overwhelming than anything he'd known with Briony, which now felt like a lifetime ago.

I can't be with her. This isn't the time.

Part of him knew that the excuse was just an excuse, that what he suddenly felt for this woman was overwhelming, severing him from his sense of himself, already changing him.

He had to sleep, and he deliberately turned away from her. No more flirting. No more dates.

But the show... He had to see her on the show.

What of it, Graham? That's your job. You always focus on the listeners. You can handle it.

In the dark, he frowned, remembering Elinor Sweet, her call about love potions and everything she'd said to Mary Anne at Giuseppi's. But Jonathan hadn't drunk the potion and Mary Anne hadn't given it to anyone else. What had she said? There was an accident.

As if in slow motion, a memory came to him. Jonathan Hale's engagement party. A broken wineglass—he'd drunk from the top half.

Ridiculous. *He* hadn't been dosed with a love potion, and he'd never believe such a thing could work.

But *was* that the accident? Graham tried to remember what had happened that night. Mary Anne had gone to get a refill for Hale, hadn't she? It had irritated him, which was why he'd teased her...

Well, if he *had* gotten the love potion, that was mildly interesting but nothing more. He'd been attracted to her from the first, though disdainful that she liked Hale. He'd never planned to get involved with her.

And he'd never, ever planned for things to go this far, but it was as if he couldn't stop himself.

Why had he slept with her? He was interested—hell, more than interested. But he'd told himself that it wouldn't change things that much. That everything would be fine.

Yet suddenly, he felt as if he was losing his moorings.

Okay, they'd made love this once. And he'd have to communicate with her.

And what are you going to say, Graham, that won't hurt her? "This is all going a little fast for me?" He was the one who'd asked her to stay the night. He was the one with the problem of suddenly wanting her beside him every night of their lives.

The truth would make no sense to her. But it made sense to him. He was in love with her, yes. But he loved his life more and wouldn't risk everything he'd so carefully rebuilt.

MARY ANNE WALKED home slowly the next morning, puzzling over Graham's behavior. After acting madly in love with her the night before, he suddenly seemed aloof. Affectionate, yes, but also aloof.

He'd seemed... Last night, she'd thought he was actually in love with her. And she had felt crazy about him. But this morning had suggested to her that she was rushing things in her own mind. She *wanted* him to be in love with her, so maybe she'd imagined him to be so.

At one point, she'd almost asked him if everything was all right, but even in her mind there'd been a desperation to those words.

You're just rushing things, Mary Anne. You spent the night together and it meant something to you, but it didn't mean the same thing to him.

She climbed the steps to her grandmother's house and unlocked the front door. As she did so, her mother came into the foyer, smiling nervously but also wringing her hands.

"Hi, Mom," Mary Anne said, her smile feeling a little sick. She knew what was coming, and she just could not deal with it right now. If she'd come home certain of Graham's love, she could have greeted her family with enthusiasm and cast off whatever her mother threw at her in the way of admonitions. Now, the thought of even *hearing* what her mother had to say exhausted her.

She was tired of pretending that life was as squeaky clean as a 1940s romance novel. She was tired of pretending that she never kissed men, let alone slept with them.

"We're going to see Nanna this morning," her mother told her. "Do you want to come? We won't mention where you were last night. I want you to know I don't approve, Mary Anne."

"I never doubted it, Mom," Mary Anne said, as cheerfully as she could manage. "And, no, I need to get some things done at the paper."

"You know if you live with a man, he's much less likely to marry you."

Mary Anne had never heard any statistics to support or disprove that assertion, but she said, "Well, I'm not living with a man, so we don't have to worry about that, do we?" Quickly she added, "I'm going to run upstairs and get ready for work."

"I hate to see you coming home in the same clothes you wore the night before."

Mary Anne pretended she hadn't heard.

She met Aunt Caroline on the stairs. "Hi, chicken," her aunt said. "We're off to the hospital. Are you coming?"

"Not this morning," Mary Anne said. "Will they let Nanna come home soon, do you think?"

"Yes, I do," Caroline said. "And we'll probably all get out of your hair, then. I know your father won't want to stay around once Mother is home."

Mary Anne gave her aunt a look of surprise. She'd never heard her father say anything negative about her grandmother. And Nanna simply pretended not to see his drinking.

Now, Caroline said cheerily, "You know. She likes to run a clean ship, your grandmother does."

Mary Anne said, "Did you see *Jaws* with my father?"

Aunt Caroline said, "I honestly don't remember anything about it, chicken."

Save me from Southern gentility! Mary Anne wanted to scream.

"He would have seen it with your mother, I'd think," her aunt continued. "But she never saw it, so there you are. Now, give me a kiss, and I'll see you later."

SHE WAS WORKING on the layout for the society page when Graham called.

He said, "Just calling to tell you that I really enjoyed you being here last night. Thank you for a wonderful evening."

"Thank you," Mary Anne said. "And ditto."

She waited for him to say something else, to suggest they get together that night, but he didn't. He just said, "Well, that's all I called to say."

"Okay," Mary Anne answered, determinedly upbeat. "I'll talk to you soon."

"Have a great day," he said.

"Thanks." He'd just made it better by calling, but it wasn't the call she'd been hoping for, a call asking her to see him again.

Don't be impatient, Mary Anne. Everything's fine.

But it didn't feel fine.

NANNA CAME HOME the next day. Contrary to Aunt Caroline's projections, her parents did not leave. Aunt Caroline, however, did.

Mary Anne discovered a strange peace in the arrangement. Her father seemed to be making an effort to curb his drinking—or at least Mary Anne did not see him drunk. She enjoyed his company, and on Thursday—the last full day her parents planned to spend in Logan—he even joined her on a bike ride.

It was also the date of her first appearance on Graham's show since they'd spent the night together, and Mary Anne was nervous. He had not called since his quick thank-you for their night together, and she couldn't even discuss her anxiety with Cameron because she wasn't ready to tell her cousin she'd slept with Graham.

Anyhow, the one time she'd talked to Cameron since their aunt's birthday, her cousin had seemed preoccupied, extremely agitated about something. When Mary Anne had asked if everything was okay, Cameron had answered vaguely, "I *think* so," then had claimed to be preoccupied with work.

Mary Anne's bike ride with her father was in weather cold enough to make Jon Clive Drew hypothesize they might see snow later that day. They turned off the highway onto a familiar dirt road used by the power company for maintaining their lines, and as they rode, Mary Anne said, "Okay, so who really went to see *Jaws?*"

She heard the slow squeak of brakes from her grandfather's bicycle, a mountain bike–style five-speed that had never been that great. Mary Anne drew to a stop, too, on her own mountain bike, and the wind whipped strands of hair from her helmet in front of her face and across her sunglasses lenses.

She forced herself to look at her father. He was staring up at the trees. Finally, he looked at her.

"Why do you ask that, Mary Anne?"

She said, "I'm sorry. Just being a jerk, I guess."

Her father shook his head and regarded her with a look that seemed compassionate.

Abruptly, Mary Anne forgave him for so many things. For all the times he'd been drunk, for the mawkish scenes of remorse. Here was her father, the real essence of her father, a man who could show keen wisdom about people and their weaknesses and their strengths. When he was wise, she wanted nothing more than his love, approval and esteem, nothing more than to feel his pride in her.

Now, he leaned on the handlebars of his bike and put his head in his hands. "Mary Anne, we *all* went to that movie. Your mother included. It's just one of those things that your mother, for reasons unknown to me and the rest of the world, does not care to admit. And she's not lying when she says she didn't see it. We were all drinking some raw stuff that Dean Milligan's brother had made, and your mother got sick as a dog. A wonder she didn't die, truth be told. All three girls stayed with a friend, and Louise had to make a phone call to your grandmother and say that's where they were staying. Your mother is mortified at the recollection."

"My mother was *drunk?*"

He straightened up and said, "And you will *never, ever* mention it to her."

Mary Anne tilted her head briefly toward the sky, trying to imagine a younger version of her mother drunk enough to be sick. Her mother, whom she'd always believed had never done anything disgraceful in her life. "Why does she act like she's never made a mistake?"

Her father bit his lip and was quiet for what felt like minutes. "I think we should all be grateful for that trait."

Mary Anne looked at him, and saw that his eyes were wet. This wasn't one of his stupid dramas, his soliloquies on how he needed divine forgiveness. This was genuine sorrow for the mistakes *he* had made. She knew exactly what he had not said.

That they all—her father and her brother and herself—should be grateful that her mother never admitted to past mistakes, because then she might admit to the biggest mistake of all. Her choice of spouse.

Instead, she stayed and loved him.

Mary Anne felt tears come to her own eyes and spontaneously leaned toward her father and embraced him. She said, "That wasn't a mistake at all, Dad."

MARY ANNE WAS IN A subdued but peaceful mood when she walked into the radio station that afternoon. The day's topic on *Life—with Dr. Graham Corbett* was Good Date/Bad Date. Mary Anne had already suggested that today's callers would probably be more interested in listening to themselves than in seeking advice, but he'd just smiled and said that the listeners would like it anyhow.

He was waiting in a brown herringbone sport coat and khaki chinos and he smiled when he saw Mary Anne, but there was an aloofness to the smile.

What have I done? she thought. She said, "Is everything all right?"

He nodded, his eyes on hers.

Minutes later, Graham was taking the first caller.

It turned out to be a show full of laughter, because so many people wanted to call in with their bad date stories. Graham yielded to the callers' direction, only occasionally talking people through "turning bad dates to good dates" and similar problems. At one point, he asked Mary Anne for her best and worst date experiences.

She described one date who had actually parked his car, removed the key from the ignition and cleaned his ear with it. Then, she decided to give credit where credit was due. "My best dates have actually occurred rather recently." She described going to Rick's with a man whose company she liked and she described a man joining her for a family dinner and helping her to escape subsequently to a peaceful environment where they could enjoy each other's company. Her face warm, she avoided Graham's eyes. "It wasn't all about champagne or jetting to Paris, but the important components were there. I felt as if I was really spending time with a friend."

There was an unradio-like pause after her words.

Then, another caller.

CHAPTER TWELVE

"YOU SLEPT WITH HIM, you're in love with him, and now he hasn't called you again and you're miserable."

It was the heart-to-heart with Cameron that Mary Anne had needed for weeks. It was almost Thanksgiving, and her interactions with Graham had been confined to the radio show and brief conversations in the studio. Finally, when Cameron had asked for the third time how things were going between Mary Anne and Jonathan— *nowhere,* because Mary Anne hadn't gone out with him again—Cameron had said, "What about Graham?" and Mary Anne had told her.

"Yes," she said in response to Cameron's summation. "Now, you and I can be the Graham Corbett Lonely Hearts Club. Or something like that."

"To be honest," Cameron said, "it's been a while since I've thought much about him."

"You mean, Bridget's potion *worked?*" Mary Anne mused, "Maybe she can make some more."

"Bridget Cureux is the Wicked Witch of the East. If no one can find a boulder to drop on her, she should be burned at the stake," Cameron hissed with sudden venom. Then, bizarrely, her tone shifted. Though still tense, she sounded otherwise almost ordinary. "Look, will you go caving with us Saturday?"

"*No* caving," Mary Anne objected, knowing Cameron was talking about her next Women of Strength outing. "Besides, it's the day after the biggest shopping day of the year, and I think I want to go to Charleston or something. Maybe I'll get trampled to death at the mall and be out of my suffering."

"Childbirth is suffering," Cameron snapped. "Everything else is just part of being female."

This was such an odd statement, even for Cameron, that Mary Anne burst out laughing.

"Oh, shut up," Cameron almost snarled back.

Mary Anne was on her cell phone but on a deserted dirt road, the same she'd traversed with her father just weeks before. She'd been riding her bike when the phone vibrated at her hip. It was mortifying to know she'd brought the stupid thing with her in the hope Graham might call—despite all evidence that he wouldn't be calling again. She looked around, saw no one, and asked Cameron, "Have you missed a period or something?"

"Yes."

All Mary Anne's pain over Graham momentarily vanished. "Who did you—" She stopped. Cameron would tell her if Cameron wanted to tell her. But if Cameron was pregnant, the terror that would provoke in her friend would surpass any heartache Mary Anne could feel over the loss of any man's affection. She understood the truism that the only help for sorrow was to care for others, to give to them. "Oh, honey. Do you really think—"

"I don't think. I *know*. Do you think I would put off five minutes finding out?"

"What can I do?" Mary Anne asked carefully. She did not ask, *What are you going to do?* Cameron was such a combination of rough-and-tough independence with marshmallow vulnerability that Mary Anne feared for her.

"You don't have to do anything—except not talk about this to *anyone*. He doesn't know."

"Who is—" Mary Anne stopped herself again, realizing at the same time that she'd now asked this twice.

"It doesn't matter. *He's* not having anything to do with it. Besides, probably a doctor will tell me my pelvis isn't big enough and I'll have a cesarean anyhow. Right?"

Mary Anne did not say *Right*. Cameron's older sister had endured the pregnancy from hell. And the biggest part of that hell had been the constant fear that she might lose the baby. And whoever *he* was, *he* probably *should* have something to do with his child. But she didn't know what to say except, "Oh, Cameron. Are you all right? Please tell me what I can do."

"You can go caving. I told you it's Big Jim's Cave. Oh, God, I think I'm going to throw up."

"You have morning sickness?"

"No! I'm terrified! Nanna and my mother are going to die of shame because I'm pregnant out of wedlock, and *I'm* going to die in childbirth."

"Won't ginger make your period come, if it's late?" Mary Anne was going back to problem one, late period.

"I'm *pregnant*," Cameron snapped. Then added, "I can't believe I told you this on your cell phone."

Implying that it would thus be broadcast throughout West Virginia, to shocked family members and the heretofore oblivious father of her child.

Mary Anne wondered how she would feel if she were pregnant with Graham Corbett's child. She asked abruptly, "Didn't you use a condom?"

"Of course we did! I should have had my tubes tied when I was thirteen years old is what I should have done."

Cameron sounded increasingly hysterical.

"Okay. I'll go caving," Mary Anne agreed.

"Look," Cameron said, making an obvious effort to sound calm, "invite him for Thanksgiving dinner. Maybe he's not calling you because he's not sure you like him."

"Oh, please. He's a grownup and he knows how to ask a woman for a date."

"It was just a thought."

"Aren't you going to tell me who—"

"We're leaving at ten, Saturday morning, and I promise it's a big cave with big passages and you won't get stuck."

LATER THAT DAY, after brief conversations with Nanna and Lucille, Mary Anne called Graham.

He answered on the first ring. "Graham Corbett."

"Hi." She sat on her bed, trembling from head to foot. The sound of his voice did not help matters. "It's Mary Anne." *Keep going, Mary Anne. Spit it out.* "I'm calling to invite you to my grandmother's house for Thanksgiving dinner."

A minute's silence. Then he said, "Actually, my mother will be visiting—"

Mary Anne didn't let him finish. "Well, we would love to have her, too."

Another pause. Finally, almost businesslike, he said, "Thank you. We'd enjoy that."

LATE THANKSGIVING MORNING, Mary Anne put on a brown wraparound dress she'd gotten at a resale shop in

New York City the previous Christmas. It was her favorite dress, sexy without making her feel overdressed. She heard a knock at the door and went to open it, getting there before Lucille.

"Surprise!"

Mary Anne stared. On the porch stood her parents, her brother, Kevin, and his girlfriend, Kendra.

The positive feelings with which she'd bid farewell to her parents so recently rushed back through her mind. She'd felt forgiving of both of them and thankful that they had done that one difficult thing of staying together, even more grateful that they'd done it without recriminations and grudges.

It was hard to call up those feelings now, however, to make them a part of *this* moment.

She managed to say, "You're back...so soon. How nice."

"We told Mother we'd come soon," Katie Drew said. "And look who came, too. Kevin met us at the airport."

"Good," Mary Anne said breathlessly, stunned, pausing to hug her brother and his girlfriend. Kevin and Kendra had lived together for three years, a fact Mary Anne's mother never mentioned except to say she wished they'd get married. As far as Mary Anne knew, her grandmother had no idea that Kevin and Kendra lived together.

The new arrivals called for another leaf in the table, and as Mary Anne and her brother accomplished this task over Lucille's protests Mary Anne thought that it was a good metaphor for life. When the unexpected happens, put another leaf in the table. And pick a tablecloth that can cover it all, the Billingham way.

Briefly, Mary Anne considered calling the Cureux

house to see if Clare or the Wicked Witch of the East—why *had* Cameron called her that?—had anything to keep her family from alienating Graham and his mother. Graham—well, he probably knew the worst. But she'd hoped to make a good impression on his mother. At least Cameron and her parents were coming, too. Maybe in the confusion, Graham's mother might miss whatever gaffes Mary Anne's mother and father made.

Cameron had been invited to the Cureux house by Paul, and when her cousin's family arrived that afternoon Mary Anne had asked her why she hadn't wanted to go.

Cameron had nearly shrieked, "Would you?"

Mary Anne murmured quietly, "Did Bridget have anything to do with...?" No need to finish that sentence.

Cameron had simply glared at her, answer enough.

At three exactly the doorbell rang, and Lucille hurried to answer it. Mary Anne's father was on his third whiskey and sitting at the piano, picking out "Dark as a Dungeon" and trying to get Kevin to sing along.

Kevin and Mary Anne sat on the couch drinking cabernet sauvignon while Cameron stuck to nonalcoholic cider. All three exchanged looks, while Kendra harmonized with Jon Clive Drew. Nanna sat in her chair beside Mary Anne's mother, who was working on needlepoint as Nanna crocheted.

Mary Anne stood to welcome Graham and his mother.

Evelyn Corbett was as tall as Mary Anne. She wore her white hair in a chignon, and her suit was the reddish-gold of an autumn leaf. Her shoes and handbag matched, and she said, "Why, hello, Mary Anne. I've so looked forward to meeting you, and I was thrilled when Graham told me your family is here, too. This is so nice."

Mary Anne introduced Graham's mother to everyone and Graham to Kevin and Kendra.

Immediately after the introductions, Jon Clive Drew said, "Kendra, this song says it like it is. That's what it's like down in the mine. You ever lose light down there, you know what dark really is."

Kevin promptly offered Graham and his mother cocktails, and Evelyn accepted a vodka tonic and a seat on the chair at the opposite end of the couch from where Nanna and Katie Drew sat.

"Now, I want to hear all about you," Evelyn said warmly to Mary Anne. "Graham says you were a magazine editor in New York City, and now you work for the paper here."

"For my sins," Mary Anne said. "I just finished one of your books. Graham gave it to me—*The View from Above*. I loved it. There were so many layers, so much feeling."

Kendra took over at the piano, and soon she and Mary Anne's father were singing "Country Roads." Mary Anne's mother said, "I love this song."

"Me, too!" exclaimed Evelyn.

And spontaneously they all began to sing, sitting in the living room. Warmth filled Mary Anne as they all sang of West Virginia.

Afterward Kendra said, "How about this one?" And she began the traditional "These Are My Mountains."

Mary Anne found with surprise that they were behaving much as she supposed other families behaved on Thanksgiving Day. In any case, it didn't matter. She'd not forgotten the lengths she'd gone to, attempting to "snare" Jonathan Hale. And she'd won his interest. But she'd never won his love, and somehow, after the mixup with the love potion, she no longer wanted to.

No, she wanted a man who loved *her,* not someone she had to make love her. Yes, she loved Graham, had begun to love him before they'd spent that one night together. But she wasn't going to try to change herself—or him—so that he would love her back.

And he seemed not to love her. His manner was friendly but slightly aloof. Once or twice when she happened to look at him she seemed to catch him staring, but then he would look away.

The conversation caught her suddenly. Cameron was saying, "Mary Anne could tell you what it's like being related to a celebrity better than I could. But, Graham, you grew up knowing what it was like to be the son of a famous author, didn't you?"

Mary Anne had no idea how the topic had come up, but it seemed that Evelyn Corbett had just named her favorite Jon Clive Drew film.

"I did," Graham said. "And I always thought it made me a little more popular. All the girls at school with me used to steal her books from the school library. In truth, I'm not sure they knew I was alive, but they were frantically curious about my mother and loved her stories."

"I'm sure they knew you were alive," Cameron answered with studied politeness and no more. She was not eating much and seemed to be fidgeting a great deal at the table.

Mary Anne found herself thinking again about Bridget Cureux and Cameron's annoyance and suddenly she knew that Cameron must have slept with Paul. *Could* she have? She'd always sworn she never would, even if he was the last man on earth.

Hmm…

Cameron said, "Mary Anne always swore she'd never marry a celebrity." She looked at neither her uncle nor her cousin as she said that.

"And *I've* reminded her," Jon Clive Drew chimed in, "that not every celebrity gives his family cause for embarrassment."

"Yes," said his wife. "Well, we don't need to talk about that."

"Isn't this cranberry sauce good?" said Nanna, as if on cue.

Mary Anne watched Graham's face, trying to read whether he was bothered by what Cameron had said. He glanced at her, his expression unreadable.

Well, her feelings *had* changed, but there was no point in mentioning now that she could marry a celebrity—one in particular.

GRAHAM TRIED NOT TO look at Mary Anne. She'd already caught him at it several times. He'd agreed to Thanksgiving dinner because at the time she'd asked, he and his mother hadn't planned anything. That was all. Weeks earlier, he'd thought that at Thanksgiving he would like his mother to meet Mary Anne. Not because he sought his mother's approval of his choice. He wasn't making a choice, wasn't entering another relationship.

Strange, though. He and Mary Anne had gotten to know each other deeply in a short time, with only a few dates. He knew her; she knew him. Even if she didn't know precisely what he'd been like when he'd lost it after Briony's death.

"What are you going to do during your time here?" Jacqueline Billingham asked his mother.

"Well, I always love to go to the state park this time of year and see the fall colors. I know it's not as brilliant at the end of November as when the leaves are still on the trees, but I love the bare branches, too."

Cameron said, "Mary Anne and I will be there this weekend, too. Caving."

"Oh, are you a spelunker, Mary Anne?" Evelyn Corbett asked gaily.

"Definitely not," Mary Anne said. "I've been assured this is a large cave and there's nowhere I can get stuck."

"I wish you girls wouldn't do that," her mother said. "It's not very safe."

"Cameron's experienced," said Jon Clive Drew.

"And Mary Anne's cautious," Mary Anne chimed in. "Not to mention, inherently terrified."

"Are you claustrophobic?" Graham asked.

"I suppose if I have a phobia, that might be it," Mary Anne mused. "But, no, I don't think I'm that scared. Do you have any phobias?"

"My heavens, yes," said his mother.

"It's not *that* bad," Graham said.

"Oh, yes, it is," Evelyn Corbett retorted. "When you were a boy, you wouldn't even go out in the garden alone to help with the weeding."

Graham blushed and looked at Mary Anne. "Snakes."

Mary Anne's mother shuddered. "I don't blame you a bit."

"As an adult," he confided, "I have worked my way up to going hiking. I just wear heavy pants and leather boots."

"Remember that black snake down in our basement the one year?" Nanna said. "Louise went down and saw it and came up to get her daddy, and when they went back down they couldn't find it at first."

Aunt Louise echoed her sister's shudder. "It had gone under the laundry. But Daddy killed it."

Graham wished the subject hadn't come up. He could do without any more snake-in-the-basement stories.

Mary Anne said abruptly, "Let's talk about something else."

"THAT WAS VERY NICE," Graham's mother said as the two of them walked home together. "I like your friend Mary Anne."

"So do I." He didn't trust himself to say more.

"Her father puts a bit away, doesn't he?"

"Oh, yes."

Back at his house, his mother removed her suit jacket and settled on the couch. She gazed across the room at the photo of Graham and Briony on the mantel and sighed.

Graham glanced at her.

"I don't suppose you meet many women here," his mother remarked.

"Are you hinting that I should marry again?"

"Of course not. That's your business, honey. I just don't want you to be lonely."

"I think I'd rather be alone than go through what I did after Briony's death."

"Well, that's a shame," she answered, "thinking that way. It hurts awfully to lose someone you love—"

"The person I lost was myself," Graham interrupted heatedly.

"But you found yourself again, now, didn't you?" she replied, unmoved by his tone. "Imagine if I'd never married your father, just because I was afraid of losing him someday. It's the silliest thing I ever heard."

Graham thought coolly of how Mary Anne had once told him that *her* mother didn't understand her. Well, she wasn't the only one whose mother didn't get the picture. He wanted to call her on the phone and tell her himself.

But he wouldn't call her. Not now. Not ever. His mother didn't understand his feelings, but he did. And he would honor them.

CHAPTER THIRTEEN

"NO TAKERS FOR CAVING at the end of November," Mary Anne said cheerfully as she and Cameron waited in her car outside the women's resource center, where Cameron had arranged for would-be cavers to meet before their outing. "Surprise, surprise."

"Give it a minute," Cameron said. "I put up lots of posters."

Mary Anne remained hopeful that no one would show and *she* wouldn't have to venture into Big Jim's Cave. The main reason she was here was to support Cameron. Well, that was the first reason. The second was to get an admission from Cameron.

Watching the entrance to the parking lot, she said, "Okay, fess up, cousin. It was Paul, wasn't it?"

"What?" Cameron's head snapped around. "What was Paul?"

Mary Anne gave her a pitying look.

Cameron said, "If you tell *anyone*…"

"You're going to tell *him,* aren't you?"

"Eventually. He's not stupid, so if he sees me at seven months it might occur to him that maybe he had something to do with it."

"My new little cousin," Mary Anne said, "is going to

be a *beautiful* child. And who knows—maybe it will be a girl with her grandmother's gifts."

"Please don't say that ever again," Cameron begged.

"I'm just kidding! Obviously, the love potion didn't work, and I doubt your getting over Graham had anything to do with whatever Bridget gave you. *And,*" Mary Anne added before Cameron could say it, "if you're going to tell me you think that little vial you drank had anything to do with your sleeping with her brother, I won't believe that, either."

"Believe what you want," Cameron snapped and reached for the door handle as a white Camry turned into the lot.

Mary Anne watched her cousin cross the lot, and the driver rolled down her window. Cameron bent to speak with her, then turned and gave Mary Anne a thumbs-up, meaning the cave trip was on.

Which was when Mary Anne saw the driver.

Angie Workman.

GRAHAM WAS RELIEVED his mother hadn't again brought up the subject of him and Briony or the advisability of marrying again—or not, as she claimed she had no interest in that end.

They'd spent Friday together shopping in downtown Logan, having lunch and coffee together and picking out some things for his guest room. The errands made him think of Mary Anne and the furnishings he'd never picked out with her because the two of them had been so keen to get into bed together.

He found himself wishing Mary Anne was along on the shopping trip.

By Saturday, however, he was almost normal again.

His mother put on casual clothes and he put on the heavy canvas pants and boots he'd mentioned at Thanksgiving—though by now all the snakes in the vicinity should be well and truly asleep—and he and Evelyn Corbett set out for the state park.

His mother said, "Let's try to do that whole Limestone Trail this year. It's just three miles. I think I can finish that, and I want to see those rock formations again."

Graham tried to remember what cave Mary Anne and Cameron were supposed to be exploring this weekend and if it was on the Limestone Trail. He had no idea, but his mother was showing a strong preference for the trail. Anyhow, he and Mary Anne still had three radio shows to complete together. It wasn't as if he was never going to see the woman. Whether he saw her or not, he would eventually get over her. That was all.

"The Limestone Trail it is."

MARY ANNE FOUND IT wasn't as awkward being with Angie Workman as she'd feared, once they were all riding to the park in Mary Anne's car. Obviously, her presence was as much of a shock to Angie as Angie's was to her.

But as they drove, Cameron queried Angie on what had attracted her to the excursion.

"Well, you hung up the sign at the Blooming Rose, and I kept looking at it. I used to love to go in caves when I was little, but I almost got lost once and my nerve sort of disappeared. I thought I'd give it another try, now, and learn safe techniques."

"Great!" Cameron said with real enthusiasm.

Mary Anne was glad she'd come, glad Cameron was doing this. Like Mary Anne, Cameron needed to get her

mind off her own problems for a while. Helping Angie
Workman learn spelunking technique—and feel stronger
within herself—was clearly just the ticket.

By the time they were all in the first room of Big Jim's
Cave, Mary Anne felt almost as comfortable with Angie
as if they'd never had a wordless tug-of-war over a man.
They were all wearing coveralls—Angie was borrowing
an extra pair of Cameron's as they were close to the same
size—and helmets and headlamps. And they were all
wearing packs, Cameron's being the heaviest. Mary Anne
had asked if it was too heavy for her cousin, but Cameron
had just laughed and given her a look that said she hoped
that was the last mention of the subject.

Cameron had a cave guide and she'd mapped their
route. "We're going to Boulder Gulch," she said, "and
there are no tight squeezes. The important thing is to be
very sure of every rock before you put your weight on it."

They started through the cave, over a dry trail already
bearing the prints of a few feet. Under Cameron's instruc-
tion, they made an effort to step in each other's tracks.

They saw a colony of bats hanging from the ceiling in
White Alley and near a small pool Angie spotted a blind
salamander. She exclaimed, "Aren't the creatures of this
world wonderful?" She was full of enthusiasm for the
cave environment, and Mary Anne remembered her
earlier thought that Angie had nothing in common with
Jonathan Hale. She still felt that way. Her dates with
Jonathan had been oriented toward watching movies and
his attempts to get her into bed. There was something distinctly spiritual about Angie.

She was still thinking of this as she followed Cameron
and Angie over the first big rocks of Boulder Gulch.

"We've got a drop on the right," Cameron said, "so be careful. There are so many crevices over there with passages close to the surface. I think they've explored…"

The rock beneath Mary Anne shifted, and she immediately tried to jump to her left, but the rock she landed on shifted, too. She fell backward, into blackness, and landed hard, with an audible crack. A wave of nausea rolled over her. The pain in her tibia was unlike anything she'd ever felt, and she vomited and after that she didn't try to move because she knew moving would cause more pain. That was when she realized her shoulder felt wrong, too. She started to move that, and the nausea returned—stronger.

There was sound around her, like cicadas. Her headlamp had come free from her helmet and the light was several feet away. She did not reach for it because if she moved she'd throw up again.

"Mary Anne?" The lights above her, blinding her, seemed to come from a distant source. It was probably only eight feet away, but it felt like a hundred.

Beside her, something moved. Something alive.

Oh, God. It was probably a cave snake or something disgusting.

The buzzing seemed to slow, then restarted.

She turned her face away from the blinding lights and saw what their beams touched.

Rattlesnakes.

Not one or two. Too many to count. Curled up together like a happy family. Mary Anne saw coils one foot from her face.

"It's winter," Cameron said from above her. "Don't move, and they won't do anything. I swear it, Mary Anne.

Remember that guy in South Africa who spent like half a year or something in a room with cobras and black mambas? Just don't move. These guys aren't even active."

"That's why they're rattling," Mary Anne said weakly.

Cameron said, "I've got a rope, and I'm going to lower it to…"

"You can't! I can't move. I think my shoulder's dislocated, and there's a boulder on my leg."

"No, there isn't," Cameron said with firm denial.

Mary Anne looked, trying to see in the dark, but she could feel the boulder. "I think there is."

"Then, I'll come down there."

"No!" Mary Anne exclaimed.

"*I* will," said Angie. "Look. I can use that crack right there."

"I'm going first," Cameron said.

"*No*," Mary Anne repeated. "Let Angie. If you come down here…"

"All right," Cameron said. "Angie, we need something to use as a lever to move the rock. I've got walking poles, but I doubt they'll be strong enough."

Angie was already climbing down to Mary Anne. Two feet above Mary Anne's level, she stopped, her headlamp sweeping the ground. It was nearly wall-to-wall snakes. "Give me a walking pole," she told Cameron. "I'm going to have to move some of these guys."

Mary Anne remembered every thought she'd ever had about Angie Workman that had underestimated the woman. She'd thought her less than intelligent, *boring,* so many things that did no justice to the courage she was showing in this moment.

It seemed to take forever, Mary Anne closing her eyes

as a snake with a body almost two inches in diameter wrapped sluggishly over the walking pole. It had to weigh a ton, but Angie slowly moved the pole over toward the darkness, depositing the snake on top of some of its fellows, who renewed their buzzing.

"Mary Anne, I'm not going to move any of the ones close to you right now."

"You guys, I'm sure I'm losing circulation in this leg. I'm afraid they're going to have to cut it off or something, and I don't think either of you can move this rock. Please go for help. I'll be fine."

Angie's light flashed up to Cameron's. She said, "You go. I'll stay with her."

Cameron went.

MARY ANNE IS GOING TO DIE. Mary Anne is going to die, and it's my fault for making her come. She came because of me, because I was stupid and got pregnant, and now she's going to die or lose her leg.

Cameron was able to run through the first passages they'd traversed—bad caving technique, but this was an emergency. Her cell phone was in her pack. It should work from the parking lot. Would anybody be at the ranger station or should she call the zoo? She'd call 911 first, and then the people at the park.

She dug her cell phone from her pack and left her pack at the cave mouth, then ran toward the parking lot, opening her phone as she went, looking for a signal.

"Wow, sister!"

She crashed into a male chest. A tall male.

Oh, God, it was Graham Corbett. The snake-a-phobe and his mother.

"Graham, there's been an accident. Mary Anne's trapped in the cave. I've got to get to a signal."

"Where is she?"

"Big Jim's. But don't go in there. You won't be able to help."

"Go," he told Cameron, and watched her sprint off, braids flying behind her underneath the climbing helmet she still wore.

"Should we help?" said his mother. "What should we do?"

"I'm going," he said, his voice seeming faint, faraway. "Cameron will come back after she calls for help." Why hadn't he asked her where in the cave? He didn't know these caves. He hadn't done any caving as a child because of a completely irrational fear that snakes would den there.

"Go ahead," his mother said. "I'll follow on my own. The cave's marked, isn't it? Don't go in there and get lost, Graham."

"No," he said and started up the trail.

When he came to Cameron's pack, he realized that he didn't even have a light. But she would have extra light sources, wouldn't she? Wasn't that one of the rules of caving?

He found a flashlight in the top pocket of her pack, switched it on and entered the cave.

He thought he could see which way the women had gone, because the footprints looked more recent down one passage.

He started that way, calling out, "Hello?"

He thought he heard voices, kept moving, and called out again.

Down a white passage with bats overhead.

Mary Anne was trapped.

Cameron actually had looked ill, and there was something disturbing about the way she'd said, "You can't help." Something factual and final.

He kept going. Called "Hello?" again.

"We're down here! I'll show you the way."

A woman's voice. Not Mary Anne's.

"I'm coming!" he called back.

He saw another light as he reached an area filled with boulders. A small female shape wearing a headlamp was coming over the boulders.

"Stay where you are," he said.

"Oh, thank God. It's a man!"

Graham had never heard anyone sing the praises of his sex so fervently. He thought he heard another voice say something else, but he couldn't tell what. "Mary Anne?" he called.

Mary Anne knew his voice. The coil beside her had moved, and she told herself that what Cameron had said was true. She was not these animals' prey. They would not recognize her as a food source. If she did not move, there was no reason for any of them to bite her.

Graham was here.

Graham *could* move the boulder.

She had a sudden vision of him refusing to come to the floor of the cave because of the snakes. *Maybe I won't love him anymore,* she thought stupidly.

"Don't shine that light in my eyes," she said.

He said nothing but moved the light, and she registered the planes of his face as something almost invisible in the dark, and she knew he was seeing the snakes.

"She's trapped under a boulder, and it's too big for me

or Cameron to move," Angie was saying. "I've been moving the snakes to make a path, but I haven't actually stepped on the floor yet. If we go down together, I can move more snakes."

"Yes."

She saw his flashlight beam find the path down the boulders to the floor, the path Angie already had been down and up twice. He handed the flashlight to her. "Give me some light, so I can see where I'm going."

And he stretched one long leg down.

HE WAS COMING. It had nothing to do with her. It was just decency. And she was down here feeling stupid and broken and hurting, and she couldn't move at all because moving would make her throw up and what if they had to cut off her leg?

Mary Anne had not cried and would not cry.

Instead, she said, "Cameron says they'll be slow because it's winter. They're really not moving much. They're just a bit noisy sometimes."

INDEED, GRAHAM NOTICED, the rattlesnakes were *very* noisy. "I won't step on you, guys," he said, trying not to think of photographs with snakes' jaws spread, two fangs thrust out in front at an angle that seemed, to him, unnatural. Supposedly, snakes struck faster than anyone could see.

Well, the fangs definitely couldn't penetrate his boots, and his canvas pants *were* sturdy.

But something curious was happening to him, something that didn't have much to do with his own *recoil* from snakes. The snakes were there, but they didn't matter. Except the big one near Mary Anne's head that was rattling like its neighbors.

Her shoulder looked strange. Angie Workman, for that was whom the small woman in the caving helmet had proven to be, was delivering a nonstop monologue. That Mary Anne thought her leg was crushed, thought her shoulder dislocated. He said, "Give me that flashlight."

When it was in his hand, he shone it on the snakes on the floor. If they didn't move, he could step between them and the pile of rocks.

He shone the light on the boulder trapping Mary Anne's leg. It was smaller than a trash can, and he knew he could lift it.

He stepped down to the ground between coiled bodies. He reached the boulder. "Baby, if I lift this, will you be able to move out from under it?"

"I don't know."

"Should I come down and move her out as you lift?" asked Angie.

Brave woman, he thought. "Yes."

"I don't think there's room," said Mary Anne. "I can do it. I'll make myself do it."

He met her eyes, trying to read her strength in them. "Okay. You've got to do it, because I don't want to put it back down on you."

"Yes," Mary Anne said, swallowing.

He came close to her, careful not to disturb her nearest neighbor. What if the snakes decided to strike as he lifted the boulder?

I have to move, Mary Anne told herself. *I have to move, no matter what.*

"I'm going to go to the right," she said. "Toward you."

"Yes."

He grabbed the rock, annoyed that it was sandy, which threatened to compromise his grip. "On three. One, two, three."

She moaned and yanked herself forward, dragging her calf toward him. Pain surrounded her and everything went black.

CHAPTER FOURTEEN

"I CAN DO IT. I can do it from this bed," Mary Anne had insisted to Jonathan Hale. "If you can figure out the phone thing so we can take callers. This is a series. I can't not do it."

Jonathan had asked her what drugs she was on. She'd had two surgeries on her foot and calf, but the doctors were optimistic.

Now the studio was her semiprivate hospital room, shared with a woman who'd trashed her knee in-line skating. Her roommate was a wildlife biologist by profession, and upon hearing Mary Anne's story, she'd promptly sent a colleague to count the rattlesnakes denning in Big Jim's Cave.

Mary Anne told Graham, who was settling in a chair not far from her bed, "I bet we're going to get challenging callers today."

The topic was Recognizing the Real Thing. This would lead up to the next two weeks: Popping the Question, and Tying the Knot.

Graham gave her a smile that was less aloof than the one she'd seen before he'd rescued her from the cave. He had not brought her flowers but had shown up the day after her first surgery with a four-foot-long rattlesnake puppet purchased at the state park zoo. Mary Anne had named it Buzz, suspecting she would become even more fond of it than she had of Flossy.

Graham had made her laugh by showing her that when he got upset, Buzz had a habit of tying himself in knots.

But she hadn't seen him since. Not till today. The show.

Jonathan was set up against the wall, and Mary Anne and Graham donned headphones to take the first caller.

"Ellen" said, "I've been dating this guy for four weeks. Every Saturday. We have this agreement. Every weekend we go to this old theater that shows black-and-white movies. We drink mint juleps and watch the movie. It's like a commitment, that we both know we're always going to be doing that on Saturday afternoons. So, I think he must be kind of serious about me, don't you?"

Graham answered that one, reminding her that her date could simply perceive her as a reliable friend and that it was impossible to tell his intentions without knowing more.

The next caller was a woman whose boyfriend had asked her to marry him. "The thing is, every time he has a girlfriend, he tries to get her to marry him, and he has been through, like, one girlfriend a year."

"Has he ever been married?" Mary Anne asked.

"Once. The divorce was epic, but it doesn't seem to have put him off romance. The thing is, it just doesn't make me feel too special since he's also asked every other woman he has ever dated to marry him."

"I hear you," Mary Anne said feelingly.

The final caller of the day identified himself as James and said, "Okay, I've had a girlfriend for three years. She's a hairdresser. She's like my best friend. We've talked about moving in together, but I know she really wants to get married. The thing is—how do I know she's the one?"

Mary Anne opened her mouth, then shut it. What could she tell this guy? She knew what made her feel as if she could marry someone, but it was something unique in her heart.

Graham said, "Well, I've heard some people say they *don't* know."

"Really?"

"But it's not like that for me," Graham answered.

"Yeah?"

Graham stared ahead of him into space, the way he did whenever formulating an especially serious answer. "For me, it's like this. Say you're really, really terrified of something. Heights. Enclosed spaces. Let's use snakes."

Mary Anne's pulse picked up. But she wouldn't let herself think. She mustn't. It would all be too painful. If she was wrong. So she mustn't think.

Anyhow, Graham wasn't looking at her. He was still staring straight ahead, concentrating on his words.

"And say the woman who has you wondering if she's the one is… Well, let's say she's caving. We know there aren't snakes in caves, but let's just say for once there are."

"Actually," James said, "I think snakes sometimes do den in caves. Anyhow, for sure there are blind snakes, cave snakes."

"Right," Graham agreed. "Anyhow, say this woman you think you like, you think you might even be a bit in love with, falls and gets stuck under a boulder."

"Okay."

Mary Anne's face felt warm. Now, she *couldn't* look at Graham, couldn't look at Jonathan, couldn't even look at the wildlife biologist in the next bed, whom she sensed was suddenly staring between her and Graham.

"She's stuck under a boulder, she's been there a while, she's afraid she's going to lose her leg. But that's not all. She is surrounded by venomous snakes." Spontaneously, Graham reached for Buzz and rattled him next to his microphone. "In fact, there's a big one right beside her head."

Mary Anne swallowed, unable to think a single word, determined *not* to think.

"And you come upon this scene. What do you do?" Graham asked.

"Well—" James said. "I'm not sure."

"Come on. Imagine it's your hairdresser girlfriend."

"Well, if it was Karen. Man, if it was Karen, I'd get down there. Screw the snakes. Excuse me, sorry I said it that way. I mean, I wouldn't care. I'd have to help her. I couldn't let her lie there."

"Dude, help is on the way. *You* don't have to go down there," Graham argued. "Someone else will be right along. You can hang out, talk her through it from a safe place."

"No way. No way. I'd get down there. I'd get that rock off her."

Graham smiled, still into the distance, as if at James, somewhere out there, listening. "There you have it, James. I think you know. Thanks for your call. This is Graham Corbett...."

As he ended the show, he finally turned his head to look at Mary Anne, then pulled his headphones off.

The wildlife biologist pushed the button for a nurse, then said, "Sir..."

Mary Anne turned. Her roommate was looking not at Graham but at Jonathan.

"Yes?" he said.

"I hate to ask you this, because I swear a lot when we do it, but I am supposed to get out of this bed and go up and down the hall. Can I talk you into keeping me company, if a nurse isn't available?" She gave Jonathan three enormous, slow, extremely obvious winks, tilting her head ever so subtly toward Mary Anne's bed.

"Right. Right. Just let me clear a path," Jonathan answered, suddenly scurrying.

THEY WERE ALONE. Maybe only for minutes. Mary Anne's family had threatened to visit.

Graham pulled his chair close to the side of the bed. Mary Anne lay back against her pillow, looking at him, trying to make herself say something that would take him off the hook, that wouldn't *force* him to do anything he might not want to do. She could say that the show had gone well. She could say that Buzz had been a nice touch. Hell, she could ask after Flossy.

She said, "You drank the love potion, Graham. *You* drank it. At Jonathan's party. You took the glass…" She let her voice trail off. "I didn't mean it to happen."

His grin broadened. "They don't work anyhow."

Mary Anne swallowed. "Good. Of course not. I knew it wouldn't. That's why I never… Well, it would have been stupid to tell you."

"Definitely." His eyes seemed to smile more completely now. He bit his bottom lip, as though choosing words. "I have the distinct feeling that your mother and grandmother and perhaps your aunt Louise and definitely the very respectable Lucille might really have something to say if you were to move in with a man to whom you weren't married."

Mary Anne tried to think what to say. Was he asking her to live with him? How did she feel about that?

A little let down. Just a little. Because…

"And," Graham went on before she could answer, "I'm feeling quite a bit more comfortable with the idea of snakes these days, but I have to admit I'm still terrified of provoking Lucille's disapproval."

Mary Anne laughed, admitting, "Me, too." *I mustn't be disappointed. I can think all this over.*

"So I think I better do it the right way."

In an athletic movement worthy of a man who could lift a boulder off an injured woman, he dropped to one knee and took her hand. "Mary Anne, will you marry me?"

She held his hand back, holding it tightly, the hand she would always want to hold. "Yes. *Yes.*"

EPILOGUE

THE LOGAN STANDARD and the Miner was open to the society page, and Bridget Cureux was gutting the season's last pumpkin on top of it. Behind her at the sink, her mother was teaching her son Nicky to peel potatoes. Across the table, Cameron McAllister, looking ill, was rolling out pie crust. Bridget's father and brother came in the door behind her, carrying a trestle bench between them. It was an antique of her mother's, which her father had refinished.

Bridget flicked pumpkin off her spoon and used the utensil to point to an item on the society page. *Mr. and Mrs. Jon Clive Drew announce…*

"And you say they don't work, Dad. Look at that."

Cameron's head snapped up. "What are you talking about?"

David Cureux squinted at the engagement announcement.

"The love potion," said Bridget. "Obviously, this is the guy who drank it."

Cameron stared rather blankly. "What makes you think that, Bridget?"

"Because it's who Mary Anne is marrying," Bridget said as if it was the most obvious thing in the world.

"She dosed Hale," said Paul dismissively. He looked thoughtful and suddenly cheered. "Score one for Dad."

"How do you know?" Bridget asked. "Were you there when he drank it? It seems to me you're underestimating our mother's powers, Paul."

"No—just your omniscience, sis."

Abruptly Cameron left the table, hurrying down the hall.

"What's with her?" asked Paul. Setting down his end of the bench, leaving it awkwardly in the middle of the room, he started toward the hall.

Bridget dug her spoon into the pumpkin, smiling a witchy smile.

*****

*Harlequin is 60 years old,
and Harlequin Blaze is celebrating!
After all, a lot can happen in 60 years,
or 60 minutes...or 60 seconds!
Find out what's going down in Blaze's
heart-stopping new miniseries,
FROM 0 TO 60!
Getting from "Hello" to "How was it?"
can happen fast....*

*Here's a sneak peek of the first book,
A LONG, HARD RIDE
by Alison Kent.
Available March 2009.*

"Is that for me?" Trey asked.

Cardin Worth cocked her head to the side and considered how much better the day already seemed. "Good morning to you, too."

When she didn't hold out the second cup of coffee for him to take, he came closer. She sipped from her heavy white mug, hiding her grin and her giddy rush of nerves behind it.

But when he stopped in front of her, she made the mistake of lowering her gaze from his face to the exposed strip of his chest. It was either give him his cup of coffee or bury her nose against him and breathe in. She remembered so clearly how he smelled. How he tasted.

She gave him his coffee.

After taking a quick gulp, he smiled and said, "Good morning, Cardin. I hope the floor wasn't too hard for you."

The hardness of the floor hadn't been the problem. She shook her head. "Are you kidding? I slept like a baby, swaddled in my sleeping bag."

"In my sleeping bag, you mean."

If he wanted to get technical, yeah. "Thanks for the loaner. It made sleeping on the floor almost bearable."

As had the warmth of his spooned body, she thought, then quickly changed the subject. "I saw you have a loaf of bread and some eggs. Would you like me to cook breakfast?"

He lowered his coffee mug slowly, his gaze as warm as the sun on her shoulders, as the ceramic heating her hands. "I didn't bring you out here to wait on me."

"You didn't bring me out here at all. I volunteered to come."

"To help me get ready for the race. Not to serve me."

"It's just breakfast, Trey. And coffee." Even if last night it had been more. Even if the way he was looking at her made her want to climb back into that sleeping bag. "I work much better when my stomach's not growling. I thought it might be the same for you."

"It is, but I'll cook. You made the coffee."

"That's because I can't work at all without caffeine."

"If I'd known that, I would've put on a pot as soon I got up."

"What time *did* you get up?" Judging by the sun's position, she swore it couldn't be any later than seven now. And, yeah, they'd agreed to start working at six.

"Maybe four?" he guessed, giving her a lazy smile.

"But it was almost two…" She let the sentence dangle, finishing the thought privately. She was quite sure he knew exactly what time they'd finally fallen asleep after he'd made love to her.

The question facing her now was where did this relationship—if you could even call it *that*—go from here?

* * * * *

You're invited to join our Tell Harlequin Reader Panel!

By joining our new reader panel you will:

- Receive Harlequin® books—they are FREE and yours to keep with no obligation to purchase anything!
- Participate in fun online surveys
- Exchange opinions and ideas with women just like you
- Have a say in our new book ideas and help us publish the best in women's fiction

In addition, you will have a chance to win great prizes and receive special gifts!
See Web site for details. Some conditions apply.
Space is limited.

To join, visit us at
www.TellHarlequin.com.

REQUEST YOUR FREE BOOKS!

2 FREE NOVELS PLUS 2 FREE GIFTS!

HARLEQUIN®

Super Romance®

Exciting, emotional, unexpected!

YES! Please send me 2 FREE Harlequin Superromance® novels and my 2 FREE gifts (gifts are worth about $10). After receiving them, if I don't wish to receive any more books, I can return the shipping statement marked "cancel." If I don't cancel, I will receive 6 brand-new novels every month and be billed just $4.69 per book in the U.S. or $5.24 per book in Canada, plus 25¢ shipping and handling per book and applicable taxes, if any*. That's a savings of close to 15% off the cover price! I understand that accepting the 2 free books and gifts places me under no obligation to buy anything. I can always return a shipment and cancel at any time. Even if I never buy another book from Harlequin, the two free books and gifts are mine to keep forever.

135 HDN EEX7 336 HDN EEYK

Name	(PLEASE PRINT)	

Address		Apt. #

City	State/Prov.	Zip/Postal Code

Signature (if under 18, a parent or guardian must sign)

Mail to the **Harlequin Reader Service:**
IN U.S.A.: P.O. Box 1867, Buffalo, NY 14240-1867
IN CANADA: P.O. Box 609, Fort Erie, Ontario L2A 5X3

Not valid to current subscribers of Harlequin Superromance books.

Want to try two free books from another line?
Call 1-800-873-8635 or visit www.morefreebooks.com.

* Terms and prices subject to change without notice. N.Y. residents add applicable sales tax. Canadian residents will be charged applicable provincial taxes and GST. Offer not valid in Quebec. This offer is limited to one order per household. All orders subject to approval. Credit or debit balances in a customer's account(s) may be offset by any other outstanding balance owed by or to the customer. Please allow 4 to 6 weeks for delivery. Offer available while quantities last.

Your Privacy: Harlequin is committed to protecting your privacy. Our Privacy Policy is available online at www.eHarlequin.com or upon request from the Reader Service. From time to time we make our lists of customers available to reputable third parties who may have a product or service of interest to you. If you would prefer we not share your name and address, please check here. ☐

HSR08R

SPECIAL EDITION

TRAVIS'S APPEAL

by *USA TODAY* bestselling author
MARIE FERRARELLA

Shana O'Reilly couldn't deny it—family lawyer
Travis Marlowe had some kind of appeal. But
as Travis handled her father's tricky estate
planning, he discovered things weren't what
they seemed in the O'Reilly clan. Would
an explosive secret leave Travis and Shana's
budding relationship in tatters?

*Available March 2009
wherever books are sold.*

The Inside Romance newsletter has a NEW look for the new year!

Same great content, brand-new look!

The Inside Romance newsletter is a FREE quarterly newsletter highlighting our upcoming series releases and promotions!

Click on the Inside Romance link on the front page of **www.eHarlequin.com** or e-mail us at insideromance@harlequin.ca to sign up to receive your FREE newsletter today!

You can also subscribe by writing to us at: HARLEQUIN BOOKS Attention: Customer Service Department P.O. Box 9057, Buffalo, NY 14269-9057

Please allow 4-6 weeks for delivery of the first issue by mail.

IRNNEW09

HARLEQUIN®
Super Romance®

COMING NEXT MONTH

Available March 10, 2009

BUNDLES of JOY

#1548 MOTHER TO BE • Tanya Michaels
9 Months Later

With a sizzling career in commercial real estate and an even hotter younger boyfriend, Delia Carlisle can't believe those two pink lines of a pregnancy test are real. She's forty-three, for Pete's sake! Suddenly Delia's not just giving birth to a baby—*everything* in her life is about to change....

#1549 CHILD'S PLAY • Cindi Myers
You, Me & the Kids

Designer Diana Shelton is not what principal Jason Benton expects when he commissions a playscape for his school. Even though he falls instantly for her—pregnancy and all—getting involved complicates this single dad's life...until he discovers love can be as simple as child's play.

#1550 SOPHIE'S SECRET • Tara Taylor Quinn
Shelter Valley Stories

For years Duane Konch and Sophie Curtis have had a secret affair. That works for them—given their difference in ages and his social status. Then Sophie gets pregnant. And now she must choose between the man she loves and the child they've created.

#1551 A NATURAL FATHER • Sarah Mayberry

Single, pregnant and in need of a business partner is not what Lucy Basso had planned. Still, things look up when hottie Dominic Bianco invests in her company. It's just too bad she can't keep her mind *on* business and *off* thoughts of how great a father he might be.

#1552 HER BEST FRIEND'S BROTHER • Kay Stockham
The Tulanes of Tennessee

Pregnant by her best friend's brother? No, this isn't happening to Shelby Brookes. That crazy—unforgettable—night with Luke Tulane was their little secret. But no way can it remain a secret now. Not with Luke insisting they meet at the altar in front of everyone!

#1553 BABY IN HER ARMS • Stella MacLean
Everlasting Love

Widow Emily Martin loves having a newborn in her arms—her own babies in the past and now her grandchild. It's all about new life...although that's a phrase she's been hearing far too often from her children, who say *she* needs to start living again. And then she finds eleven love letters from her husband....

HSRCNMBPA0209